HOSPITAL IN THE MOUNTAINS

After a terrible car accident, Nurse Jill Sinclair accompanies her injured brother to an Austrian clinic where Baron von Reimer hopes to repair his injuries. But the Doctor Baron is such an attractive man that Jill soon finds herself in an impossible situation . . .

For Emma and David

HOSPITAL IN
THE MOUNTAINS

BY

JEAN EVANS

MILLS & BOON LIMITED
London . Sydney . Toronto

First published in Great Britain 1981
by Mills & Boon Limited,
15–16 Brook's Mews,
London W1A 1DR

© Jean Evans 1981

Australian copyright 1981
Philippine copyright 1981

ISBN 0 263 73567 2

Set in Monophoto Baskerville 11 on 12½ pt

*Made and printed in Great Britain by
Richard Clay (The Chaucer Press) Ltd.,
Bungay, Suffolk*

CHAPTER ONE

THE car's windscreen wipers moved sluggishly under the weight of the snow as it drifted towards them like huge moths, picked out in the arc of the headlights.

Jill Sinclair frowned uneasily in the passenger seat. If it got much worse they would have to abandon all thoughts of getting to their parents' home. She cast a side-long glance at her brother and saw the look of concentration on his face. It had been snowing quite lightly when he picked her up at the main gate of St Kits where she worked as a Staff Nurse. She had questioned then the wisdom of making the twenty mile journey and was now seriously regretting that she had allowed herself to be persuaded.

Her gaze shifted from the road to Martin's face again. The fact that he had taken the driver's seat of the faithful old red mini was no reflection upon her own capabilities as a driver, she knew that. She had passed her test three years ago just after she qualified as an SRN whereas Martin was still flushed from having just acquired his own licence. She realised now that she should have been firmer and insisted on driving in conditions like these but he had seemed to need something into which to divert his restlessness. She saw the tightening of his hands on the steering wheel and was struck again by the slim sensitivity of them. They were the hands of a musician. It was ironic how things had turned out, she thought. Their parents had always cherished the hope that one day Martin would follow in their father's footsteps and become a GP. His obvious abhorrence of the idea had been a disappointment to them both and not even her own decision to train as a nurse had completely made up for it.

In a way she understood their concern. They had wanted security for their children, security which medicine seemed to offer and music did not. Only the growing knowledge that Martin's talents as a pianist bordered upon genius had gradually begun to reconcile them to something they didn't understand.

Perhaps that accounted for his temperament too, she thought as, with a growing sense of alarm, her gaze went to the speedometer. Working in a busy Casualty department she saw road accident victims being brought in every day.

'For heaven's sake, Martin, slow down. I'd rather we were late getting there than didn't arrive at all.' Tiredness gave an edge to her voice. She turned to peer out into the blackness, seeing nothing but swirls of snow beating against the headlamps. 'Why don't we stop somewhere and phone to say we'll be a bit late. They'll expect it on a night like this. What's the hurry anyway. You phoned me out of the blue and came rushing up from London . . .'

He fumbled for a pack of cigarettes. She took it

quickly, lit one for him and passed it over. 'I'd rather we pressed on if you don't mind.'

She shook her head, thinking longingly of the cup of coffee she had denied herself because she had already been late getting off duty. 'It's alright, but slow down.'

She took a cigarette herself. She didn't often smoke but it kept her hands occupied, kept her from snatching at the wheel. In the darkness she studied him through a haze of smoke. In looks they were really quite different, for where he had chestnut-coloured hair her own was fair and curled against the collar of her navy uniform coat. There hadn't even been time to change into her everyday clothes. Both did have grey-green eyes, but it was in temperament that they were poles apart. She had always been the placid one and her training as a nurse had taught her a sense of discipline. One didn't argue with Sister, she thought wryly. But Martin's temper was of the quick-silver variety, flaring in an instant and fading to leave him regretting it in the next.

The small car lurched sickeningly on the narrow country road and he swore under his breath. He slowed a little but not enough to make her feel any happier. Even in the dark she could sense the tension in him.

'Don't you think it might help if you tell me what it's all about,' she said, smiling. 'Or does it have to be a full-scale family gathering before you tell the secret?'

She saw the faint flicker of a grin as he half turned.

'What makes you think there's any secret?'

'Because you were exactly like this when you were picked for the school football team and you've been dying to tell me whatever it is from the minute I set foot in this car.'

He stubbed out his cigarette in the ash tray, half-smiling again. 'Well, if you must know, I've been offered a scholarship, at the Steckler Institute in New York.'

She drew in her breath, staring at him in amazement. 'But . . . the Steckler is world famous. All the top musicians begin there.'

'I know,' he said softly. 'Can you imagine what it means to me, to be able to study music for a whole year with the very best. It's the chance of a lifetime, Jill. Something I've always dreamed of, in fact I still can't believe it.'

Jill clasped her hands. 'Oh Martin, that's marvellous. When do you go?'

As his gaze flickered towards her again she saw the sudden hint of strain in his good-looking face. 'That's just it. I leave in three days time.'

She released her breath slowly. 'So soon?'

'Don't you see, that's why I have to tell the folks tonight. I won't have another chance. There are so many arrangements to make, the flight, packing.'

'Yes, I see that.'

'The question is,' his hand half rose from the wheel, 'how will Dad take it? He's never really understood about my music, has he?'

She bit her lip. 'Only because he's a bit old-fashioned and wants what most fathers want, I suppose, for his son to follow in his own footsteps. After all, he retires in a few years and I suppose he always had an idea of handing the practice over to you.'

He shrugged. 'I'm afraid I let him down by not inheriting his love of medicine.'

'It's not something you can force. Either you love it or you don't. I think Dad only wants what's best for you.'

'And you mean that for every successful concert pianist there are a hundred who never make the grade,' he said grimly. 'Well, let's face it, he may be right. I may not be good enough.'

Her hand rose. 'But don't you at least owe it to yourself to find out?'

'That's what I hoped you'd say.' He turned towards her and in the same instant she saw the lights of an oncoming car as they swept round a narrow bend in the road. A scream died in her throat. She saw Martin grappling with the wheel, heard the screech of brakes before the car swerved sickeningly.

It was all over in a matter of seconds. She was thrown violently sideways. Something made sharp contact with her head and as she fell she was vaguely aware of Martin, beneath her, his face ashen. He groaned before his eyes closed.

'Oh no. No.' She knew she was mumbling incoherently but her brain seemed numb. She tried to move but her limbs wouldn't respond and she felt sick.

The lights of the other car illuminated the scene,

like some stage play, she thought hysterically. Through the shattered windscreen she could see it, lying at a crazy angle, half in the ditch. She should get out, see who was injured. Try and get help.

It was the snow, gusting through the broken glass on to her face which roused her. There was no way of telling how long she had been unconscious, probably only a matter of seconds. A trickle of blood ran warmly towards her eye. She brushed it away. By a sheer effort of will she managed to lift an arm and moved carefully. Martin groaned and she noticed more blood though she couldn't tell whether it was his or her own.

She was gripped by a momentary sense of panic until, miraculously, her training began to take over. Her fingers felt, shakily, for a pulse. It was weak but at least he was alive. Somehow she managed to drag a car rug from the back seat and tucked it round him. He was lying on one arm and she didn't want to move him too much. The other she checked for fracture but as far as she could tell there was none. The best thing she could do would be to get help and as quickly as possible before they all froze to death.

Somehow she managed to open the door and climb out. She was surprised to discover that she was trembling violently and her legs threatened to give way until she clung to the car door for support. The cold hit her forcibly and she gasped as she looked around and had to wait for a wave of dizziness to subside before she was able to move again.

The snow crunched beneath the soles of her flat,

sensible shoes and she thanked God for them as she groped her way round the car and managed to open the door on the driver's side. Martin slumped towards her. She caught his weight and somehow managed to extricate him from the distorted tangle of the steering wheel.

Dragging off her coat she covered him then sat on the edge of the seat as dizziness surged over her again. She musn't pass out, now now. She had to get help. But her legs wouldn't move and her body felt numb with cold.

She wasn't aware of the tall figure until a man's voice spoke. She tried to push away the hands which were moving over her body, probing gently. Why wouldn't he just leave her alone to sleep? Then her face was tilted upwards suddenly and she stared dumbly into a pair of incredibly dark eyes.

'What the devil were you doing, you little fool. Don't you know better than to drive at that sort of speed in conditions like these?'

She stared at him and felt the resentment stir in her. How dare he? Just who did he think he was? Her brain vaguely registered that his voice held some faint trace of an accent which she couldn't place, but it was his appearance, his manner which held her, even in those moments of confusion. There was an arrogance about him. She saw it in the expression in his grey eyes and felt it in the firm grip of his hands as they held her. He was tall and slim almost to the point of gauntness.

At her protest he released her abruptly. 'You're

alright,' he said tersely. 'A knock on the head but nothing serious. Pull yourself together.'

Resentfully she drew herself up, unaware of the tears trembling on the brink of her lashes. On the point of arguing, she remembered Martin.

'My brother. He's hurt, badly I think.'

The man was already on his knees beside him. She watched, incapable of movement as he seemed to make a quick and expert examination. Something in the actions roused her.

'I think you should leave him alone,' she said stiffly. 'It isn't wise to move an accident victim until you know what damage has been done.'

The stranger's fair head rose and the cold, grey eyes regarded her intently. 'What do you suggest? That we leave him here to freeze to death?' Without giving her time to reply he bent again. 'His legs are not broken but he needs to be taken to a hospital.'

She fixed him with a cool stare. 'I am a trained nurse.'

The dark, arrogant gaze met hers and flicked over the uniform. 'So I see. Well in that case you should know better than to stand here arguing. There is another passenger, in my car, who needs urgent medical help. I think it's serious so let's not have any hysterics. I'd hate to have to slap that pretty face.' His expression almost seemed to belie the words but before she could speak he was lifting Martin. It must have taken a considerable amount of strength but he moved as if the lifeless body in his arms were weightless.

He carried him towards the other car leaving her no choice but to follow. It was all like a nightmare. She walked blindly behind the tall figure and watched as he lay him on the back seat of the large car before he moved quickly to the front passenger door.

For the first time then she saw the girl, slumped against the windscreen, and gasped as she moved involuntarily forward. Unthinkingly her fingers gently brushed aside honey-blonde hair to reveal a deep gash on the girl's temple. Blood had matted the hair, her skin was cold and clammy, her breathing was shallow.

'It's bad,' she breathed. 'You're right, she does need urgent help.'

The stranger nodded grimly. 'There's concussion, possibly a skull fracture, but I'm more worried about possible internal injuries. She came to just for a second and said she couldn't feel her legs.'

Jill's gaze flew up to meet his. She had worked in Casualty long enough to know what that might mean.

'You think there might be spinal injury?' It didn't occur to her to wonder why she assumed that he would know. From the first he had taken control. His actions, she saw now, were those of someone who knew exactly what he was doing and suddenly she was only too glad to let him take over, even if she didn't like his manner. She felt too weary to argue and her head was spinning.

As he straightened up she noticed that he was

wearing a dinner jacket. It suited his tall, rugged figure. He was really quite handsome, she thought in a detached way, her eyes being drawn to the wing of greying hair which fell towards his eyes and she felt an incredible urge to brush it away. She shivered uncontrollably as the snow soaked through her thin dress and, without a word, he took off the jacket, draping it about her shoulders. She could smell the subtle trace of after-shave and she swayed a little as a feeling of warmth and comfort swept over her.

'Don't you faint on me now, young lady.' His voice brought her sharply back to full consciousness. With an effort she managed to get a grip on herself.

'Don't worry,' she said snappishly, 'I'm not the fainting type. Anyway, I am a nurse. A good one,' she added defiantly. 'I see this sort of thing in Casualty every day.'

The dark glance seemed to mock her. 'But it's rather different when you happen to be personally involved.' He took her by the arm and, with the arrogance she had begun to recognise as typical of him, made her get into the driver's seat. 'I'm afraid I'm going to have to leave you alone for a while.' He saw her large green eyes flicker in alarm. 'I'm sorry but someone must go for help and it looks as if I'm unanimously elected.'

She put her hands to her face. She was still shaking and supposed it must be shock but, suddenly, the thought of being left, filled her with panic.

'I'll be as quick as I can,' he said softly. 'Just keep

an eye on both of them.' He bent close to the girl again and she saw his lips brush against her forehead before he moved a strand of the long hair from her cheek. He had large hands, slim yet incredibly strong and at the same time capable of the gentleness she saw now. His mouth was taut and she saw the expression in his eyes. He was in love with the girl. His wife? There was no ring on her slender hand. Fiancée perhaps? Whoever she was she was beautiful but Jill also knew that if she didn't get help soon she would be dead.

'I'll be fine,' she managed to say. 'I won't pass out.'

'Good. I thought you had more spirit.' For a moment he stared at her and she felt the colour return to her cheeks. He nodded. 'Your brother may come round soon. Keep him quiet and still, and if Helga recovers consciousness, for God's sake don't make any attempt to move her.'

'I can cope. Don't worry, just get back as quickly as you can.' Dimly her mind registered the girl's name. She clutched his jacket round her, glad of its warmth. She must keep calm, for Martin's sake and for the girl's.

A strong hand closed for an instant over her own and she started, feeling tears prick at her eyes. Then he was gone. She watched him walk away, silhouetted against the car's headlights and a feeling of desolation swept over her.

She must have drifted into semi-consciousness for when she opened her eyes she was cold and Martin was groaning. Flicking a cigarette lighter she was able to see by her watch that it was nearly two hours since the stranger had left. A long time. Too long. Suppose he had lost his way?

Martin was coming round but seemed too dazed to be able to understand what was happening. She reassured him as best she could, covering him with the car rug and was relieved to see him drift off to sleep again. But it was the girl, Helga, who gave her real cause for concern.

After what seemed an eternity she heard and then saw the ambulance approaching and felt a surge of relief. She climbed stiffly out of the car as she saw the man come towards her and, staring up at him, she tried to speak calmly:

'I'm worried about the . . . your fiancée. She came round once but only for a second or two. I asked if she had any pain and she said there was none, none at all, that she couldn't feel her legs.' She gave the report as if to a doctor on the ward. He listened gravely and nodded before leaving her to supervise the ambulance men as they brought stretchers and began moving the girl and Martin to the waiting vehicle.

It was all accomplished surprisingly quickly and yet Jill knew she was still trembling from reaction. She was hardly aware of the man at her side until he spoke.

'We'd better get you to hospital too. You're suffering from shock.'

She tried to protest that there was no need, but

before she knew what was happening he had lifted her in his arms and was carrying her to the car and put her in the passenger seat.

Suddenly it was too much effort to argue. Her head was spinning and she was vaguely conscious of the handsome face looking down into hers. For some reason her heart was thudding wildly as she lay within the protective circle of his arms, before she fell into unconsciousness at last.

A nurse hurried to meet the ambulance as the stretchers were lifted out. The stranger's sleek, black car drew to a halt behind it and Jill roused herself, struggling out to watch helplessly as they were wheeled through the swing doors and into Casualty.

Jill followed. Even in shock, her brain registered the fact that Casualty was busy, having one of those peaks to which she had become so accustomed when they got the drunken drivers, the drug over-doses and sometimes the down-and-outs who just wanted somewhere warm to spend a couple of hours.

All this she saw in a kind of blur. Had it not been for the steadying hand under her elbow she knew she would probably have fallen. Delayed shock they called it but she had never really understood, until now, what it felt like.

Martin was being wheeled into one of the cubicles. She shook off the stranger's hand and went to walk beside her brother. She was appalled by the whiteness of his face and her fingers felt the thready pulse in his wrist. As if he realised she was there, his eyes flickered open briefly.

'Where am I?' His hand went up to shade his eyes.

'Don't worry. Everything will be fine.' She heard herself making the sort of response she would to any patient. 'There's been an accident but you're in good hands.'

She felt relief well up as the white-coated figure of Keith Hammond, the Senior Registrar, arrived on the scene. She knew him well. He was young but a very capable doctor. Martin couldn't be in better hands. To her surprise, however, he exchanged a few words with the stranger and she was given the distinct impression that they knew each other. Keith was actually smiling and shaking his hand and then, to her complete amazement, the stranger issued a command to the hovering student nurse and Jill watched incredulous as the girl hurried away to return with a trolley. Surely he couldn't be going . . .

Grim-faced, he removed the expensive-looking silk scarf he was wearing and bent over the girl, gently cutting away the fabric of her evening gown where it had adhered to a wound. He worked fast and deftly, concentrating every ounce of his energies into the task before him. Jill guessed that he wasn't even aware of the small audience which had gathered round. He swabbed the head wound with antiseptic. A nurse wheeled in the transfusion equipment. The whole thing was done smoothly and, Jill had to admit, with a professionalism she had rarely seen before even in this hospital with its high reputation.

Grudgingly she found herself watching the handsome face, seeing the faint shadows of exhaustion, the firm set of his mouth. He was younger than she had first imagined, probably in his mid-thirties. It was probably his air of complete self-assurance which had fooled her. Even here, little by little he had assumed control, giving orders in that quiet but firm tone which, for some reason, grated on her nerves.

He had turned his attention to Martin, working over him with Keith Hammond. She moved instinctively forward but then a hand closed over hers and she knew she was trembling violently. Exhaustion flooded over her and she felt ridiculously close to tears as she looked up.

'There is nothing you can do here, Nurse. Go and sit down before you fall down. We have our hands sufficiently full without having to waste valuable time reviving you.'

She gasped, her face stinging with colour as she stared at him through a mist of tears before she turned and fled. How dare he? Just who did he think he was?

Outside in the corridor she paced up and down, frustrated by the desire to go back and see what was happening and at the same time horribly aware that he had been right. She knew from experience that distraught relatives often made the doctor's work more difficult. But this was different, this was Martin in there.

She was handed a cup of tea by one of the student

nurses, a girl she had often worked with, but just at this moment Jill felt in no mood to chat.

It seemed an eternity before the curtains were drawn back against the cubicles and she rose quickly to her feet, conscious of the sudden dryness in her mouth.

Keith Hammond was talking to the man at his side. 'It's fortunate you were here, Herr Doctor,' she heard him say. 'At least now there is a chance.'

Jill brushed a hand through her hair. 'What ... what is it? How bad ...?' Unthinkingly she addressed her words to the stranger, seeing the weariness in his eyes and remembering only now that he had been on his feet for hours. For a moment he studied her and something in his expression filled her with a sense of chilly unease as she realised it was anger she saw there.

'We have done all we can for now. The best thing you can do is to go and get some rest. I'm sure doctor will prescribe a mild sedative.' The dark eyes searched her face, seeing the pinched whiteness. 'I would guess that you are suffering a mild concussion yourself. A remarkably lucky escape under the circumstances.'

She fell back, confused by the coldness in his voice until she remembered the girl he had been travelling with. He must love her very much, she thought with a strange sense of desolation. But then, she loved Martin too.

And then the awful realisation hit her. Someone would be held responsible for the accident and

Martin had been driving. They had been talking, far too absorbed in the marvellous news about the scholarship. . . . Her gaze flew up and she had the chilling feeling that he had just read her thoughts as the cold, challenging stare met hers.

Before she could utter a sound he said brusquely, 'Go to bed, Nurse. I promise you that your brother is in no danger.' Then he turned on his heel, leaving her standing beside the Senior Registrar.

Anger burst forth, tinged with the shock she had suffered. 'Just who does he think he is?' Her fists clenched.

Keith stared at her. 'You mean you really don't know?'

'I wouldn't be asking if I did, would I?'

He whistled softly through his teeth. 'Well then, my dear girl, you should. That is Dr Bruno von Reimer. One of the world's leading neurologists. In fact he is Baron von Reimer. His family are very wealthy Austrians. He has a private clinic over there.'

'I see. One of those rich ones, in it for the money and the prestige,' she said bitterly and flushed as Keith frowned.

'Actually, no he isn't. He's over here to lecture on the latest techniques in his particular field. I've heard him once before and he's good. Perhaps you of all people should be glad that he is.'

Jill lowered her head, ashamed of her cynicism. 'I'm sorry. That was unfair. It's just that something about Herr Bruno von Reimer sets my teeth on edge.'

'I dare say he's worried sick and he has a right to be,' Keith reminded her quietly. 'The girl who was with him came off worse. She's being taken to Intensive Care now. It looks as if there might be some serious spinal injury. There's a possibility she may never walk again, though of course at this stage it's not easy to be positive.' He stared after the stranger's retreating figure. 'One thing's for sure, if she ever recovers consciousness she couldn't be in better hands. But I'll tell you this, I wouldn't like to be on the receiving end if I was responsible for what happened.'

CHAPTER TWO

WAKING from an uneasy sleep, it had been some seconds before memory returned, bringing with it all the horror and a feeling of sickness in the pit of her stomach.

She had been told to stay in bed but habit died hard and she got up, slowly, conscious of the throbbing in her head and the fact that her knees felt distinctly wobbly. Looking in the mirror, Jill saw the livid bruise discolouring her temple where she must have hit it in the crash. By tomorrow it would be all shades of blue and yellow but then, as Bruno von Reimer had so scathingly reminded her, she had escaped amazingly lightly, physically at least.

The mere act of putting on the pale mauve uniform of a Staff Nurse with its crisp white apron and cuffs calmed her a little. She fastened the belt, remembering the ambition she had nurtured from her very first day at St Kits, which was to eventually wear the coveted navy belt and silver buckle worn by the sisters. Somehow, at this moment, that ambition seemed unlikely ever to come to fulfilment. It was as if, overnight, her career hung in the balance, threatened by the feelings of helplessness she had wrestled with throughout the night. She had been next to useless at a time of crisis. She had allowed her fears for Martin to supercede her duties to another patient.

Her face was pale, making her eyes seem huge as they stared back at her from the mirror. She had thought she had a vocation. It had taken someone like Bruno von Reimer to show her the full extent of her inadequacy. Pinning the dainty, frilled cap into place on her curls she left the Nurses' Home and walked quickly towards Intensive Care. Sister Bartlett sat at her desk, a neat little figure in navy blue with starched collar and cuffs, a pleated white cap perched upon iron-grey hair. The night report book lay open on the desk before her and she consulted it for a moment before considering Jill, who stood before her, hands clasped against her apron.

'I would be grateful if I could see the patient, if only for a few seconds, Sister.' She explained, as briefly as possible, her own involvement and Sister nodded.

'I have been told a few of the details of course, Nurse. Unfortunately, I don't think that your seeing Miss Klammer would serve much purpose.'

'She isn't . . . worse?'

'No, Nurse, but her condition remains critical.' Sister flicked the pages of the report book. 'She regained consciousness briefly but had a very restless night. Doctor gave her a mild sedative and will be seeing her again this morning of course. But I'm bound to say, she would not recognise you, or anyone at this stage.' She rose to her feet consulting the fob-watch she wore on her apron. 'My advice to you, Nurse, would be that you return to your duties. I understand you are in Casualty?'

'Yes, Sister.'

'Well, then, I'm sure you must be needed and there is nothing you can do here. By this evening there may well be more news. We may possibly have the results of some of the tests by then.' She frowned. 'I must say it seems a tragedy. Such a young woman and so pretty. But then these cases always are. I believe she was to be married in a few months too.'

Jill left the office with her mind in a whirl. Until now she hadn't had time to consider the implications of what had happened but at this moment they came to her in full force and she felt physically sick as she thought of Martin and the effect this must have upon him. She wondered if he had been told about the girl yet. If so, he must be feeling pretty desperate.

She hurried to Men's Medical and after a brief word of explanation to Sister was allowed to see him for a few minutes. She entered the side ward where he had been put and found him still asleep. Standing beside the bed seeing the pale face and the stray lock of hair which peeped from under the head bandage, she thought how terribly young and vulnerable he looked, and her heart lurched sickeningly. She was about to turn and leave when his lashes fluttered and he saw her. He frowned then smiled weakly.

'Hi! What the devil's been going on?' He moved his head carefully to study his surroundings. 'How did I end up here?'

She reached for his hand and held it firmly, forcing herself to speak cheerfully. 'Hullo there, troublemaker. We had a bit of an accident. Don't you remember?'

She saw his brow furrow and he brushed his uninjured hand against his brow. Her heart missed a beat.

'Sorry. I know it's ridiculous but the last thing I remember is phoning you to say I had to get home to see the folks . . .' His voice faded and she saw a new expression steal into his eyes. 'The scholarship. Oh my God. My hand.' He stared in horror at the splint which encased the fingers of his left hand.

Jill swallowed the lump in her throat. 'You hit it a little too hard in the crash. Your head too.' Her eyes scanned his white face with a feeling of dread. 'Don't you remember anything?'

He shook his head against the pillows and covered his eyes with his arm.

'Not a thing. Was it bad?' His eyes flickered open again. 'You weren't injured?'

'No.' She shook her head but he must have sensed her unease.

'Someone else. Oh God, there wasn't someone else?'

She nodded, tight-lipped. 'I'm afraid so. There was another car. A girl passenger was injured. We don't really know how badly yet but you're not to worry. What you have to do is to concentrate on getting yourself well again.'

Through the glass partition which separated them from the ward, she could see Sister gently beckoning her away. She released his hand gently. 'Look, I have to go now. I'm supposed to be on duty but they let me see you for a few minutes. I'll come back later this evening.'

He stared at her and she could see that he was already fighting against sleep. She tiptoed towards the door but as she reached it he said softly, 'I don't understand it, Jill. You're such a careful driver.'

She turned, feeling as if her heart had frozen suddenly in her breast. Her mouth opened then she closed it again quickly upon the denial she had been about to make. Martin was asleep again and she left the ward feeling as if she had just walked into a living nightmare. He believed that she had been re-sponsible for the crash and she could never bring herself to tell him the truth.

She walked on to Casualty, aware of the curious glances cast in her direction but there was a flap on and they were all too busy and too pleased to have her help to comment.

Somehow she managed to deal with her work, glad in a way to be kept too busy to think properly. She helped others to deal with a road crash victim and tried not to see that the young man who had come off his motor-bike was about the same age as Martin. He was unconscious and in a bad way. Student Nurse Johnson hurried into the cubicle wheeling a fresh oxygen cylinder as Jill handed an opthalmoscope to the Registrar and, at Sister's command, began to cut away a blood-soaked trouser leg. The young man was wheeled away to Men's Surgical and Jill turned automatically to deal with a child's sprained ankle. After that she was required to assist with a very frightened elderly patient who had fallen on the ice and was in great pain, probably suffering from a fractured hip as well as the inevitable shock which was usually so much more intense in the elderly.

It was only when a brief lull came that she left the cubicle. Drawing the curtains back and pausing, she brushed a hand wearily against her forehead as a wave of dizziness swept over her.

The voice, speaking sharply from behind her, sent her spinning round to stare into the frowning features of Bruno von Reimer. He took the kidney dish she was carrying firmly from her fingers, handing it to a passing Student Nurse who took it, casting a curious glance in their direction as he steered Jill peremptorily towards Sister's Office.

'Doctor . . . I am on duty,' she protested. The use of his professional title brought the colour to her face as she recognised her folly in not having guessed that he was no amateur last night. She struggled to free herself.

'I fully appreciate that, Nurse.' His eyes met those of Sister who, with a placidity which far belied her usual manner, miraculously gathered up her papers and left them alone. Jill gasped as he stood, barring the doorway thus preventing her escape and she backed away, putting the desk between herself and him. He was taller than she had imagined and his hair, now that she saw it in daylight, was fair except for the faint touches of grey at his temple. He was in fact handsome, her brain registered it almost unwillingly, with his aquiline nose and a mouth which was at once sensitive yet strong. For an instant a vivid picture of him cradling his fiancée in his arms with loving gentleness came to her and she felt a sense of sudden inexplicable desolation sweep over her. It was banished when he broke the silence.

'You were ordered to remain in bed, Nurse. Why, then, are you on duty?'

The cool gaze was fixed unrelentingly on her and she found herself clasping her hands together as if she were a raw probationer again, being reprimanded by Sister. The effect this man had on her was unfair. Her chin rose, defiantly.

'I am perfectly well . . . Herr Doktor . . . Baron . . .' Her voice trailed away helplessly and he made no attempt to ease her confusion.

'Are you in the habit of disobeying orders, Nurse. Perhaps you feel that you know better than your superiors?'

Her cheeks burned. 'I am quite capable of carrying on with my duties, Doctor, and you must have seen that we are already short of staff, particularly in Casualty. Since I am not ill . . .' Her hands rose, her air of confidence vanishing like mist as he continued to stare at her. 'Besides, I couldn't have rested.'

His mouth twisted sardonically. 'Could it be guilty conscience, Nurse?'

She gasped. 'What do you mean. Why should I feel guilty?'

His dark eyes narrowed, scanning her face. 'I find it incredible that you dare even ask such a question, Nurse. What in the devil possessed you to drive at such speed in those conditions?'

She stared in total disbelief, too stunned for the moment even to speak. Surely *he* couldn't think her responsible for the crash. Yet even as a denial rose she bit it back recognising the implications it would have. To tell him the truth would mean having to betray Martin and, even as her brain struggled to find some way through the nightmare, she knew that he had every reason to believe the guilt was hers. By the time he reached the car she had somehow managed to get Martin out and on to the ground, and she had been half sitting in the driver's seat, the ignition keys clutched in her hand. She recalled now that some instinct had made her remove them in case of a petrol leakage.

She bit her lip. How could she speak in her own defence even to protect herself from the cold anger she saw in his eyes.

'I'm glad you don't try to deny your responsibility,' he said.

Her stomach tightened. 'How can I?' She looked up and surprised some expression in his eyes before it vanished. Contempt? Pity? No, surely not that. A man like Bruno von Reimer was incapable of it. 'What do you mean to do?' She forced herself to ask. 'I suppose the police should have been informed.'

His hand dismissed that sharply as he turned away to stare in silence out of the window until she began to think he had forgotten her presence.

Her sense of agitation increased. Whatever he intended, she wished he would get on with it. Or was this all part of the punishment?

'I . . . I understand that your fiancée is in Intensive Care. Can you at least tell me if there is any news yet?'

She saw the fine lines of exhaustion etched into his face as he turned to look at her. 'At this stage it is too early to make any positive prediction.' His long hands gestured. 'It could be the spine itself which is injured. It could equally well be the nerves. Until a more thorough examination has been carried out it is impossible to say and I don't like guesses. Whatever the outcome, we must face the possibility that Helga may never walk again and you, Nurse, will have to live with the knowledge that the blame is yours. Do you think you will be able to live with it?'

She blanched at the savagery of the words, her eyes misting with tears. 'I am truly sorry.'

'Sorry.' He spat the word. 'Can you have any notion of what it will mean to a girl like Helga who has been able to ski, to skate, to dance . . .' He broke off, battling for self-control, yet there was no way she could escape the contempt she saw in his eyes. Nor could she blame him for feeling as he did when the woman he was to have married had been turned into a helpless cripple and he believed her to be responsible. Whatever happened she must make absolutely sure that Martin never learned the truth.

'You attended to my brother's injuries,' she said, conscious of the awful dryness of her mouth. 'Under the circumstances I am immensely grateful.'

His eyes narrowed. 'I did what I would have done for anyone, regardless of circumstances.'

She nodded miserably. 'Can you tell me how bad it is?'

Incredibly, the dark gaze softened as if he suddenly became aware of her own concern. 'There were no internal injuries. X-ray showed a slight skull fracture and there was severe bruising to the ribs. I'm rather more concerned about the damage to the tendons in the left hand.'

She swayed as if he had dealt her a physical blow. Surely fate couldn't be so cruel?

'Are you alright, Nurse?' A cool hand rested on her arm and she drew herself up.

'Yes. I . . . What sort of damage? How serious is it?'

His brows drew together in a frown. 'Until the superficial bruising has gone down it would be impossible to say for sure but I'm afraid there is a distinct possibility that your brother may never have total mobility of his fingers again in that hand.'

A wave of sickness hit her. Her voice came to her as if from a great distance away. 'Surely something can be done?'

'As a nurse you should know the old adage of always looking to the positive and, in any case, even if the worst should happen, he will still be able to lead an almost normal life. Patients adapt, Nurse, even to having to change the habits of a lifetime.'

But not Martin, she thought. His hands *are* his life, his whole future.

'I could be wrong,' he reminded her, studying her face.

Somehow she doubted it. Even in her short knowledge of him she couldn't imagine him making a mistake. There was a ruthlessness about him, a ruthlessness strangely at odds with the gentleness she had witnessed when he tried to comfort the girl he was to marry.

She moved towards the door and for some reason the injustice of the contempt she saw in his eyes hurt. Yet she could say nothing, do nothing to put it right. She didn't stop to ask herself why it should be so important that he knew the truth.

At the door she paused. 'I want you to know that

I would give anything if I could turn the clock back and none of this nightmare had happened. Or if it could be me lying injured there instead of your fiancée.' It was difficult to speak with that piercing glance watching her. 'If there was anything I could do, anything at all, I would do it, I want you to believe that.'

He was standing very close and she lowered her head rather than look at him.

'Words are cheap, Nurse.'

'I meant them nonetheless,' she said stiffly.

'I hope so, because it's highly likely that I shall call upon you to do just that, Nurse.' And before she could ask what he meant he had reached across to jerk the door open and walked briskly out to leave her staring after him.

A desperate need to be kept busy drove her to throw herself back into the hectic routine of the Casualty Department. Sister Randall had suggested that she take a few days off and go home but she had refused. The last thing she needed now was time to think. Instead, she had phoned her parents and reassured them about Martin. There had seemed little point in alarming them with too many details of the accident. Even so her mother had passed the telephone over to her husband so that Jill could explain properly. To her relief she had been able to persuade him that there was little point in travelling all the way to the hospital in such bad conditions to see him.

'He's behaving like a bear with a sore head now that he's beginning to feel better,' she had joked. 'The nurses are threatening to isolate him so that they can get on with some work.'

The lies, or half lies didn't come easily. Martin's condition had improved. He was getting over the skull fracture and his bruised ribs were healing. She knew that the real cause of irritability was the uncertainty about the damage to his hand.

She went along to Clarke Ward during her break to find him sitting in a chair at the window, lost deep in thought. Catching only a glimpse of her uniform he mistook her for one of the ward nurses and said sharply, 'Look, why don't you just leave me alone. I'm sick and tired of being messed around. Just tell me when I can get out of here, that's all I want.'

Her heart went out to him. Fear and uncertainty were often the worst enemies in hospital and she had been a nurse long enough to recognise the symptoms for what they were.

She forced herself to smile as she went towards him and rumpled his hair.

'So that's how you treat your nurses is it.' To her dismay he drew away.

'What's the matter? Come to sympathise? I suppose they've told you I may never be able to play the piano again and you've been sent to dish out a few soft words. Well, save it. Why don't you just go away and leave me alone.'

She was shocked by the bitterness in his voice, by

the change in him. Even more by the look of defeat in his eyes.

'These things take time you know. Aren't you assuming the worst and giving up a little early?'

He turned away. 'For God's sake don't you start humouring me. I've had enough from that chap Reimer. What's the matter, are you falling for the handsome doctor like everyone else round here seems to be?'

'Don't be ridiculous,' she said quickly, almost too quickly. 'If you must know, he's the most unpleasant man it has ever been my misfortune to meet. And, in any case, he is already engaged to be married, to the young girl who was injured in the crash.'

For a moment he had the grace to look ashamed but not for long. She saw the sullen look return.

'Well, don't treat me like a child, not you of all people. You know what that scholarship means to me. It's the chance of a lifetime.' He was holding her wrist and she flinched at the strength of his grip.

'But surely they will hold a place for you?'

His look silenced her. 'Why in God's name did this have to happen to me. It's so unfair.'

'You mustn't let it make you bitter.'

His mouth twisted as he looked at her. 'Why? Don't I have the right? Ironic isn't it that you were the only one to get off scot free. There's no justice is there?'

She stared at him in shocked disbelief, searching desperately for an answer when a voice spoke from the doorway. Her glance flew to the figure of Bruno von Reimer, her heart thudding uncomfortably as she wondered how long he had been standing there, listening. But if he heard anything it wasn't apparent in the cool expression as he came towards them. His gaze flicked questioningly over her white face and, suddenly, she couldn't bear him to see the tears which were welling up. Biting her lip she fled past him, hearing him say something but not knowing what as the door closed behind her.

The door of the linen cupboard opened and she spun round to see him standing there. Angrily, she tried to brush the tears from her face knowing that her eyes were red and hating that he should see her like this.

He crossed the narrow space between them in a stride and she gasped as his hands gripped her shoulders as he swung her to face him.

'Why the devil didn't you tell me?' he demanded angrily, shaking her until she had no choice but to look at him. A tremor ran through her.

'I don't know what you mean.'

'I think you do. Why the devil didn't you tell me about your brother's music, the scholarship?'

Her struggles merely seemed to increase the steady pressure of his hands. 'Why?' she demanded. What difference would it have made? As you so rightly reminded me, I was to blame for what happened. Well don't worry, I expect nothing from you. If there is anything that can be done for Martin, any treatment which will enable him to play again, I'll get it without your help.'

She heard his sharp intake of breath and was vividly aware of his closeness, of the strength of him. The urge to stop fighting him, a desire to be drawn close overwhelmed her until common sense returned and she drew herself up sharply, too stunned by the betrayal of her own emotions to be able to speak.

'Is that really what you think of me?' he demanded. 'That I could be so vindictive, so inhuman?'

Was it what she believed? Before she could interpret the look on his face or knew what he intended, he had drawn her towards him, his hand uptilting her chin as his mouth came down over hers. His lips were hard, demanding. For an instant she was too astonished to react then, as shock receded, she became aware only of a desire to return his kiss. His hands, strong yet incredibly gentle drew her closer and, like a traitor, her mouth responded to his. Then, suddenly, she knew that this was crazy and wrong and with a low moan she tried to thrust him away. How could she have allowed herself to forget even for a moment that he was engaged to another woman.

'No.' She twisted her head away and was released abruptly. For a long moment he stared at her then his mouth curled with such contempt that she shivered. 'I was right,' she murmured, rubbing a hand across her mouth. 'You are inhuman.'

She tried to move away but his hand was on her arm, his vice-like grip hurting her but he made no attempt to release her. She brushed quickly at the tears which filled her eyes and he flung her away.

'You're right and I'll do anything, anything to repay you for what you've done. Remember that, Nurse, because where you are concerned I have no conscience. You deserve all you get.'

The words stabbed at her like a knife and she stared at him bleakly.

'How you must love her.' Her voice was little more than a whisper. 'And how much you must hate me.'

Some expression flickered briefly across his face but she didn't stop to interpret it as she pushed blindly past him. He made no move to prevent her and she fled towards the nurses' cloakroom, glad there were no curious faces to see her in such a dishevelled state.

Once safe inside, she leaned against the door and closed her eyes. It was only then that she realised she was trembling. She pressed a hand to her mouth where the pressure of his lips still remained and it was as if a cold wave washed over her.

Crossing to the wash basin she splashed cold water on to her face and stared at her reflection in the mirror. Her features were ashen as, gradually now, she was forced to accept the bitter truth. She had wanted to be kissed by him. Those few brief seconds in his arms had aroused in her emotions such as she had never known before. But it was ludicrous, she told her reflection as her hands trembled against her face. She hated him. But why, then, did her eyes look back at her, mirroring such uncertainty.

She didn't see him for the rest of the day and was glad. She needed time to bring her confused emotions under control. What had happened to her, to all her training which should have made it so easy? She moved through her tasks efficiently but mechanically, glad of anything which kept her occupied until she could go off duty. But when she finally did so, gathering her cape about her as she hurried across to the Nurses' Home, it was as if Bruno von Reimer's words were still ringing in her ears and she knew that there was nothing, nothing she could do to escape him.

She spent a near sleepless night and woke next morning feeling even more exhausted. She reported for duty having steeled herself to the inevitable meeting only to find, to her chagrin, that there was no sign of his familiar figure and, perversely, she felt cheated. After all, as she chided herself, they were two adult people and she wanted the air cleared between them, even if it meant she must lose her job, give up nursing altogether.

The thought was pushed away for the present however as she quickened her step and began to check the dressing trolleys. This morning of all mornings the Casualty Department was even more noisy and the pace hectic from the moment she had set foot in the door. Going about her work she didn't notice time passing. There wasn't even time for a tea break but that didn't worry her. She had learned to accept that when necessary such luxuries must be foregone.

She had just come out of one of the cubicles and

was directing a patient towards X-ray when she became aware of Sister, beckoning her to the small office. With a frown she automatically checked that her cap was straight and smoothed her apron before presenting herself at the desk, her mind seeking in vain for something she might have done, or omitted to do, which could conceivably have earned her a reprimand. But she could think of nothing. A new thought occurred to her and her heart skipped a beat. Perhaps it was something to do with the accident.

'Yes, Sister?'

'Ah, sit down, Nurse.'

Jill obeyed, barely able to conceal her surprise. Sister Drummond was no stickler for formality but on the rare occasions in the past when Jill had been summoned to the office, she had remained standing.

The telephone rang and she waited patiently as Sister dealt with the call before turning at last to the duty lists lying in front of her on the desk. She frowned and looked up, her glance silently approving the neat appearance of the girl sitting before her.

'I'm afraid I'm going to have to move you from Casualty, Staff Nurse. Needless to say it will cause a lot of inconvenience and I'm not at all happy about it but it seems I have no choice.'

Jill's eyes widened and she swallowed hard. 'Oh no. But why, Sister? Is there ... have there been any complaints about my work?'

Sister Drummond levelled her gaze at Jill. 'Not at all, Nurse. On the contrary I shall be extremely sorry to lose you. Casualty isn't everyone's cup of tea but you seem to have settled to it remarkably well. Your work has always been most satisfactory. You can be quite sure that had it been otherwise I would have told you about it soon enough.' Her thin lips quivered, but Jill missed the hint of a smile. 'I had hoped you would be with us for some time yet, in fact your three month period isn't up for another five weeks.' Her gaze strayed to the list and Jill clenched her hands in her lap.

'Then what is it, Sister? Why must I be moved?'

'As to that, Nurse, you must realise that mine is only a limited authority.' Sister rose to her feet and crossed to stand at the glass partition through which she could see the entire Casualty Department.

'I can only tell you that you are required for specialling duties.' She turned, her dark head neat and still very attractive despite her nearing retirement. 'I understand you have done it before.'

Jill frowned. 'Yes, Sister, though only once.'

'Well, Mr von Reimer is obviously quite satisfied with your qualifications to nurse Miss Klammer.'

A sense of dismay swept the colour from Jill's face. 'You mean . . . Mr von Reimer has asked for me?' Panic rose. 'But surely someone else could do it, Sister? I enjoy my work here in Casualty and it isn't as if I have any particular capabilities . . .'

'I'm well aware of your capabilities, Nurse, just as I'm sure you must be aware that I cannot challenge

41

Mr von Reimer's decision.' Her features relaxed a little and she sighed. 'I did suggest, after all I am as loathe to lose a good nurse as you are to go, but whatever one's personal feelings may be, Mr von Reimer is a brilliant neurologist and surgeon and his decisions are not made without a purpose.'

Jill felt her stomach tighten. She didn't doubt that this particular decision was made with a purpose, a purpose to make her suffer.

'Perhaps he feels,' Sister went on, 'that your personal involvement in this particular case can be put to some good effect. I understand that your brother was also involved.'

'Yes, Sister.' Jill sat rigidly in the chair wishing her brain would stop racing so that she could think calmly. 'Perhaps I could speak to Mr von Reimer?'

Sister Drummond was studying the lists again. 'I'm afraid that won't be possible. Oh, but of course you wouldn't know, he flew back to Austria last night and we don't expect him back for several days at least. It seems he had some urgent business to attend to at his private clinic over there.' She frowned, her long fingers flicking at the pages she held. 'I've managed to make arrangements to have you replaced here on Casualty, not that it was easy. We'll have to take someone from another ward. I don't like doing it, they are all short-staffed, but it can't be helped. You'll have time to write your report and put Staff Nurse Manriqué in the picture. She's coming over from Women's Surgical and this will be her first spell in Casualty.'

Jill rose to her feet. 'You mean I'm to go at once, Sister?'

'I'm afraid so.' Sister Drummond consulted her fob watch. 'Straight after lunch in fact. I suggest you get something to eat as soon as you've finished clearing up here. Nurse Manriqué will be over in about an hour. Apparently Mr von Reimer feels it will be beneficial to his patient to have one nurse in attendance as much as possible, so that she will become accustomed to you.'

'Yes, Sister.' Jill left the office in a daze and made her way back to Casualty where she began clearing up. It hardly seemed possible that any of this was happening. Her mouth tightened angrily. She had enjoyed working on Casualty then along came the arrogant Bruno von Reimer and with a mere lift of his hand he was able to put an end to it all.

She bent over a young child just admitted after a road accident and smiled reassuringly, explaining what was going to happen, that a few stitches would be necessary in the cut on his knee. She moved and spoke automatically but it was as if a heavy weight had suddenly taken the place of her heart.

Had Bruno von Reimer even considered what would happen when his fiancée learned, as inevitably she must, that Jill was supposedly responsible for the very accident which had brought her to St Kits? It was all so unfair. There was absolutely no way in which she could defend herself and it was almost as if the wretched man was taking advantage of the fact.

She was walking softly along the corridor towards the Nurses' Common Room, her mind too engrossed to be aware of anything save her immediate problems, when a figure loomed up before her, barring her path. She looked up with a frown of annoyance which vanished as she saw Keith Hammond smiling down at her.

'Hi! Why the face like a thunder-cloud?'

She tried to respond but failed miserably. Somehow the events of the past couple of days were catching up on her and she felt tired and tearful, not at all like her usual self.

Keith's hand tilted her chin up and he brushed a stray curl of hair from her eyes, frowning. 'What is it?'

She swallowed hard and had to subdue the impulse to throw herself into his arms. Not that Keith would have minded but to have Sister come upon such a touching little scene would have put the finishing touch to an otherwise perfectly unsatisfactory day.

She sighed. 'It's nothing really, but I'm being moved to special the girl who was brought in after the accident.'

'Von Reimer's patient you mean?'

She nodded. 'I wouldn't mind so much but I enjoyed Casualty.'

'I enjoyed it too, having you there.' With a swift glance over his shoulder he bent and kissed her. 'But actually you're quite privileged you know. Oh, but you are.' He dismissed her wry laughter. 'Von

Reimer's no fool. He wouldn't make a decision like that, ask for you, unless he knew exactly what he was doing.'

'Oh, I'm sure he knows precisely what he's doing.' Jill murmured and shivered as a sudden chill seemed to creep down her spine. 'Look, I must go. I have to be up at the Unit in fifteen minutes.'

'What about our date tonight?'

'Oh no, I'd completely forgotten,' she admitted. In fact, she had never felt less like going out, not even with Keith whose company she always enjoyed. Then she saw the disappointment on his face and relented. Anyway, it might even do her good to get away. 'It's okay. I'll meet you as usual.' And she hurried away to snatch a quick cup of coffee before spending the remainder of the morning putting the young Spanish nurse who was to take her place, in the picture.

There would have been time for a quick lunch but she decided to skip it, knowing that her stomach wouldn't be able to tolerate food anyway. She made her way instead up to the Intensive Care Unit where Sister Fraser greeted her arrival with a smile of approval. 'You're early, Nurse.' She was an attractive woman, Jill thought, with her auburn hair neatly coiled under her cap and a slim figure which was emphasised by the neat, dark blue uniform.

'Yes, Sister, I gave lunch a miss as a matter of fact.'

'Not very wise, Nurse,' the gentle Scots accent chided. 'Specialling takes it out of you, as you'll find out soon enough. You've come up from Casualty haven't you?'

'Yes, Sister.'

'Well, the pace may not be as hectic up here but you'll find that constant alertness to even the slightest changes in the patient's condition, a constant check on pulse, temperature, respiration, all that sort of thing, can be quite exhausting. Specialling means just that, Nurse. Constant vigilance. Being there, just in case.'

'Yes, I realise that, Sister.'

'Good.'

Jill glanced into the small unit where her patient lay in the narrow bed with all the necessary equipment surrounding her. It gave her something of a shock to see it. Until now she had felt detached. At the time of the accident everything had happened so quickly and was still a kind of blur. But now she was made only too vividly aware of the pale face and a mass of blonde hair beneath the bandages.

Her mouth felt suddenly dry. She dreaded going in there. She couldn't do it and surely not even Bruno von Reimer could force her? What if she were to go straight to the Senior Nursing Officer and offer her resignation? But even as she thought it she knew she wouldn't do it. It would be the coward's way out and no matter where the real blame for that accident lay, this girl needed help and she was the one who could give it, atone in some way for what had happened. It even seemed fitting. The girl must get well again, must marry the man she loved. Jill felt her hands shake.

'If you'd like to go in,' Sister was saying. 'You can take over from Staff Raymond.'

Jill entered the unit acknowledging the dark haired young nurse who nodded and smiled in her direction. She was making the usual routine checks and Jill stood quietly as she did so, looking round the small room. A chair had been placed close to the bed. On the other side of the patient an oxygen cylinder stood in readiness for any emergency although, at this moment, she was breathing easily and her colour was reasonably good.

Nurse Raymond checked the drip and then, satisfied that all was functioning normally, turned at last to Jill. 'There, that's done.'

'How is she?'

Anne Raymond finished filling in the chart and handed it to Jill. 'I'd say there is an improvement,' she said softly. 'Doctor seems quite pleased although of course the paralysis is still the major problem. Of course, as you know, there can be so many causes but all the tests are being done.'

'Have there been any results yet?' Jill managed to ask and saw the girl's quick glance of curiosity.

'Oh, but of course, you were involved weren't you? Well, yes, we've had a few but nothing conclusive unfortunately. The only consolation is that there doesn't appear to be any fracture. The blood vessels at the base of the spine are badly bruised and swollen.' Her dark lashes flickered as she looked at Jill. 'It's going to be quite some time before we really know the full extent of the damage. It may not be as bad as it seems.'

'No.' Jill swallowed the lump in her throat. 'I just hope it isn't.'

'The important thing is to keep the patient as cheerful as possible. Not easy I know but it's so easy for them to give way to depression once the more superficial effects of the accident begin to wear off.' She looked down at the patient. 'She's had a sedative to help her sleep. I'll leave you to it now. I'm off to lunch, then over to Women's Medical. You know what to do and there's a bell if you should need to summon help, or Sister is always close by. I doubt if it will be necessary. As I say, the immediate danger seems to be over. It's the long term we have to deal with and, unfortunately, in some of these cases that can literally mean long-term. I must say it seems a tragedy. She's so young, so pretty.'

'And engaged to be married,' Jill said hoarsely.

'Oh? I didn't know that. Still, at least you know she couldn't be in better hands.' She gathered up her papers and pushed her pen into her pocket. 'Mr von Reimer has been visiting her every day. He spends hours just sitting beside the bed and talking to her, even though most of the time she isn't even aware of him being there.'

'I hadn't realised.'

'Well, there's no reason why you should. But it's true and I'm sure it has helped. If anyone can give her the will to get well again I think he can. She's lucky to have someone who cares so much.'

'Yes, she is,' Jill said dully, feeling the ache in her heart yet again. Involuntarily she felt the colour rush to her cheeks. It was as if she only had to think of him and he was there like a physical presence, so strong that she felt she had only to turn her head and he would be there, watching, silently accusing.

Anger mingled suddenly with her depression. It was all so unfair. If only she could tell him the truth, that she wasn't to blame. But that wasn't possible and even if it were it would make no difference. He loved this girl and she needed him. She didn't stop to ask herself why she should care so much what his opinion of her was.

'I can leave you to cope then?'

Jill started. 'Oh yes. I was just wondering how long Mr von Reimer will be away.'

'No one seems to know. The Herr Doktor is obviously a law unto himself but at least you won't have him breathing down your neck for a while.' She consulted her watch and frowned. 'Lord, I'm due in Women's Med. I'll be lucky if I get any lunch today, the cafeteria's bound to be crowded. I'll leave you to it then but I'm sure everything will be quite straightforward. The worst is over. The real problem will be how she adapts to the possibility of not being able to walk again and, frankly, if it comes to that, I wouldn't like to be the one who has to tell her.'

Jill stared at her in dismay. 'Of course, she doesn't know.'

Staff eyed her with the kind of look she usually reserved for young students. 'Well, hardly. I mean it's not even certain but I imagine if it should become necessary Mr von Reimer will break the news to her himself. He'll have to sooner or later because she's going to start asking questions. Let's just hope that by the time that happens we'll have some answers.'

Watching her bustle away, Jill moved mechanically around the small unit, familiarising herself with the equipment and her patient's progress. The notes were detailed though as yet brief. She made the routine checks and added her own notes to the chart and report book. Anything rather than give herself time to think. But the thoughts came racing in just the same.

There was no doubt in her mind at all now but that Bruno von Reimer had insisted upon her being moved here purely as a means of exacting his revenge. He wanted her to be here, to see the pain he believed she had inflicted. Her hand went to her mouth and her lips quivered. Even the kiss had been part of the punishment and incredibly she had played right into his hands for he must have been aware of the emotions he had roused in her. She covered her face with her hands, shamed by the memory of those feelings and, above all, the knowledge that he had such power over her that she had allowed herself even for a moment to forget that he was engaged to be married. Oh, what an unlooked for victory her reaction must have given him, she thought bitterly. Now he thought her cheap as well. She would never be able to look him in the eyes again.

Her thoughts made uncomfortable companions as the hours passed slowly and, by the time she finally went off duty, she was not only physically but mentally exhausted.

Sister had been right about the difference in routine between Intensive Care and Casualty, as she soon discovered. Her previous assignment here had been a brief one, nursing a patient who had just undergone a serious operation, but now she found time hanging heavily. She missed the noise and bustle of Casualty and even the regular checks and observation of her patient still left her with too much time to think so that she was pleased to be able to escape for a few hours when her relief came to take over. Except that there was no real escape. There was still Martin.

She changed out of her uniform into her everyday clothes thinking that perhaps the sight of her as an ordinary visitor might cheer him a little. But the truth was that she was dreading seeing him again. He had recovered well from his concussion and the shock of the accident but gradually she had been appalled to find in him a growing resentment over the injury to his hand which was directed entirely at herself.

She put on a dress of soft wool in a shade of green which had always been particularly becoming to her, except that at this moment it seemed to do nothing but enhance the shadows under her eyes and the lack of colour in her cheeks. She shrugged and made

51

her way to the hospital shop where she bought chocolates and magazines before she went in to see him. Her mouth was framed into a smile as she entered the ward but her heart sank as she saw no answering response in Martin.

'Hullo there.' She kissed his cheek and felt him move imperceptibly away. 'I'm sorry I couldn't get here any sooner.'

He stared sullenly. 'You don't have to spend your spare time visiting me, you know. After all I'm not ill and there must be far better things you have to do with your off duty.'

She forced herself to speak lightly. 'I know I don't have to come, but I wanted to.' Her trained glance studied him carefully. 'You're looking better. Here, I brought you these.'

'Am I?' He made no attempt to touch the chocolates or the magazines and she put them on his locker trying not to feel too hurt by his manner. Ironically, believing as he did that she was to blame only made the injustice of it all even more difficult to bear.

She made conversation for a while but his replies were so abrupt that she soon realised she was wasting her time. Perhaps it might have been better if she hadn't come.

'Is there anything else you'd like me to bring?'

His mouth tightened. 'Look, Jill, all I'm interested in is when I can get out of here. Have they said anything to you because no one tells me anything?'

'No, of course I don't know anything, Martin,'

she replied in a quiet voice. 'If I did don't you think I'd tell you?'

'Would you?' His glance rose, sharply. 'Or are you still hoping for a miracle as I am?'

The bitterness in his voice shook her. 'I don't know what you mean.' She rose to her feet knowing her face was white as she faced him. 'No one is keeping anything from you, Martin. It's just that these things take time.'

'Oh for pity's sake, spare me that, Jill. What kind of a fool do you take me for? You know time is the one thing I don't have and if I'm not to have my music either then the sooner I know about it, the sooner I can try and learn to live with it, if that's possible.'

Her hand reached out to him but she withdrew it when she saw him flinch. 'I do know what it means to you, but there are other things, Martin, you must believe that.'

'Not for me,' he said savagely. 'Music is my life or so I thought. But then, it's easy for you. You're not the one who stands to lose everything.'

Her throat ached as she looked at him. 'No, I suppose you're right.' Why couldn't he remember? But then, even if he did, what difference would it make if he were still to lose his music? She was simply being selfish, wanted to ease her own burden.

'At least nothing is definite yet,' she forced herself to say. 'What does the doctor say?'

'Not much. What can he say? That's just it, they're all so damned non-commital about my future. I haven't even seen that chap von Reimer for a couple of days. I suppose he's washed his hands of the whole thing too.'

'You mean . . . he's been here to see you?' Her voice shook but he didn't notice anything wrong.

'Of course. He examined my hand. Why?'

'Oh, nothing.' Her brain raced in confusion. What possible reason could Bruno von Reimer have for concerning himself with Martin's case. 'As a matter of fact I happen to know he had to return to Austria for a few days, to the private clinic he has out there. But he'll be back.'

The frown momentarily left Martin's face. 'Good. I must say he seems a decent enough chap even if he didn't tell me anything about this.' The sullenness was there again as he looked at his injured hand then at Jill. 'What about the girl?' His brow furrowed. 'There was a girl, I didn't dream it?'

'Yes there was.' She reassured him quickly, alarmed by the sudden stricken look in his face. 'She is making progress . . .'

'Progress. Words. Nothing but meaningless bloody words.'

Jill rose slowly to her feet unsure of herself and his changing mood. Clearly the accident had affected him more deeply than she had imagined.

'They may be only words, but they are true, Martin. She is making progress, and so are you. If only you can learn to be patient.'

He didn't even bother to answer. He turned his

head away, covering his eyes with his hand as if he couldn't bear to see her any longer. He looked so young and so helpless that for a moment she longed to go to him, to be able to offer some comfort. But there was nothing she could say or do. She was the last person he wanted.

'I'll leave you to rest. Would you like me to come again?' He didn't answer or even look up as she moved towards the door and left.

CHAPTER THREE

THE following day was Jill's day off and after another near-sleepless night she decided the best thing would be to get away from the hospital completely for a while. It was easy enough to tell herself she wouldn't even think about Bruno von Reimer, but she had only to walk along one of the corridors and her heart would lurch sickeningly each time she saw a white-coated figure coming towards her.

'I haven't been home since the accident,' she told her friend, Staff Cooper as they walked across to the Nurses' Home together. 'I've been phoning my parents and keeping them in the picture as much as possible without wanting to alarm them but I suppose it's time I talked to them properly.'

'But what about your car?'

Jill grimaced. 'That will be off the road for days,

weeks, I dare say. But in any case I'll take the bus. It's safer.'

The weather improved and the roads were clear when she made the journey to her parents' home. She sat by the window, staring out over the fields where small pockets of snow still lay and without even being aware of it her thoughts conjured up Bruno von Reimer. It must have been an association of ideas she supposed, her lips tightening resentfully as he intruded even now. She had been to Austria, once. It had been several years ago but even now the memory of it stayed vividly with her. She had loved the majestic splendour of the mountains and the snow, the pine trees and the bitingly clear air, the freedom and yet at the same time the hint of cruelty in the towering peaks. She could imagine Bruno von Reimer in such a setting. He was worthy of it, she thought angrily. Cold as ice, glacial even! But then, out of the mists of her mind came another image, that of Helga, the girl he loved, standing beside him. Except that she may never stand again.

Jill shivered and turned up the collar of her coat. Suddenly she found herself wondering at the wisdom of her decision to come home. She hadn't even thought seriously about what she would tell her parents and the problem was still with her when the bus finally came to a halt and she got out to begin the trudge through the snow which still lay out on the narrow country track towards the picturesque cottage where they lived.

The moment she opened the door and heard their

welcome she knew she had been right however and only later, as she sat before the great roaring fire, chatting and eating hot, buttered scones did she realise just how great the strain of the past days had been. Exhaustion washed over her and her mother's keen eyes saw it and the stifled yawns.

'Can't you take some leave, dear,' she said, refilling Jill's cup and handing it to her. 'You work so hard. It might do you good to get away for a few days and you know your old room is always ready.'

Jill managed to smile. There was nothing she would have liked better than to escape but whether from the hospital or Bruno von Reimer, or simply her own tangled emotions she didn't know.

'I wish I could but at the moment it's out of the question. Perhaps later. It depends on . . . several things.'

Her mother's gaze flickered up from the teapot. She was a small woman, still attractive in a delicate sort of way. 'Everything is alright, dear. I mean . . . the accident. We did want to come over but the roads were terrible. You know how it is once the snow settles. We might be in Siberia . . .'

Jill laughed. 'Honestly, Mother, there was nothing you could have done and Martin will be fine. At least . . .' She saw her father studying her and knew that she had to tell them as much as she could. 'Well there is some doubt about the injury to his hand.' She saw her mother's quick look of concern. 'It's too early to say yet but, well there is a possibility that he may not be able to play the piano again.'

Dr Sinclair's spoon clattered into his saucer and she saw the shock on his face.

'But why didn't you let us know?'

Jill stared down at her cup. 'I wanted to, but on the other hand I didn't want to worry you needlessly. I'm sorry, perhaps I shouldn't have said anything even now, after all, it may be perfectly alright.'

To her surprise her mother received the news in a far different light. Almost as if it came as a relief.

'Well, dear, you know we had always hoped Martin would get over that idea. I mean . . . music.' She frowned and looked at her husband. 'It was never quite what we had hoped for. Perhaps now he will settle to something more serious.'

For the first time in her life Jill understood just what Martin had been up against, why he had been so reluctant to break the news about the scholarship to them, or at least to their mother. She had to force herself to bite back the angry words which rose to her lips, conscious of her father watching her closely.

'Is it really as bad as that, Jill?'

She shrugged. 'As I said, we don't know yet.'

'But how is Martin taking it?'

'Very badly, naturally.' Her voice shook. She couldn't bring herself to tell them all of it, not yet.

She put her cup on the table and rose quickly to her feet. 'I can't stay long. I'll go up and collect a few books from Martin's room. I thought one or two of his favourites might help to cheer him up.'

'Oh yes, dear, you do that.' Her mother smiled.

Jill was glad to escape. She hurried upstairs and

after finding the books took them to her own bedroom. It was kept just as she had left it, always waiting for her whenever she could get home and its familiarity drew her now. She sat on the bed and pressed a hand to her head. If only she could get away from the hospital. The last few days had been like a nightmare to which there seemed no end.

A gentle tap at the door brought her up with a start and she saw her father standing there. Out of habit he sucked the stem of his old pipe and tapped the bowl against his hand now as he smiled.

'Can you spare a minute before you have to rush off again,' he said. 'I'd like to talk. We so rarely seem to get the chance these days.'

'Of course I can.' She held the door open. 'I've another half hour before I need to catch my bus.'

'I suppose you do have to go back tonight?'

'I'm afraid so.'

'Oh well.' He sat on her bed looking round the room before his gaze settled on her pale face. 'It's a long way to come, Jill, for so brief a visit.'

She forced a laugh. 'I thought it was about time. Anyway, it's nice to have a change of atmosphere occasionally, you ought to be able to understand that. Much as I love my work there are times when I need to wash the smell of antiseptic out of my hair and think of something else besides bedpans and injections.'

The answering laughter she saw on his lips didn't somehow reach his eyes. 'There's more to it than that though, isn't there? Something's worrying you, something you haven't told us.' He stared at his pipe.

'Is it that you can't talk about it or don't want to? I'd always thought we were pretty close and could share most things.'

She tried to swallow the sudden lump in her throat. 'It isn't that I don't want to . . .'

'Then what? Is it really so bad?'

Suddenly, despite all her good intentions, her eyes filled with tears and she turned away. 'It's the accident. It was a bit more involved than I told you on the phone. I was afraid of worrying Mother.'

He grunted. 'Yes, I was afraid that might be it. She does mean well you know.'

Her lips quivered and she sat beside him, staring at her hands in her lap. 'Of course I know. It's just that it's all so involved. You see . . . well on the night of the accident Martin was on his way here to tell you that he had been awarded a year's scholarship in America.' Her eyes were turned to him, full of helplessness. 'Oh Dad, don't you see, it would have been the chance of a lifetime and now it's all been snatched away.' She had to clasp her hands together to stop them shaking and her father was silent for a moment.

'I know you thought your mother was a little . . . insensitive. She didn't mean to be but are you absolutely sure that she is wrong?' He stayed her as she began to protest. 'Oh, don't misunderstand me. Just ask yourself is it possible that Martin may learn to accept the situation if the worst should happen?'

She shook her head miserably. 'It isn't even quite that simple. I'm afraid there's more to it. You see

Martin believes...' she drew in a breath, 'he believes that I was responsible for the accident.'

She saw the stunned expression in her father's eyes. 'And you weren't?'

She met his gaze. 'No. Martin was driving. It just happened that I managed to get him out of the car and it looked...' Her hand rose. 'Well, Martin doesn't remember anything and you must see that I can't tell him.'

'But what about the chap, von Reimer you said his name was over the phone. The police, surely?'

She shook her head. 'No. Don't ask me what happened, it was all so confused. But there was a passenger in his car, his fiancée, and he doesn't want her involved in all the sordid business of a court case. Dad, she may never walk again.'

His expression was grim as he rose to his feet. 'What do you intend doing.'

Her eyes widened. 'What can I do?'

'Does von Reimer know the truth?'

'No.' She said sharply. 'And he must never know. Don't you see, Martin has enough to bear, I don't think he could take any more.'

'And what about you?'

She faced him miserably. 'I don't know, except that I came out of it best of all, physically at least, and this seems to be the least I can do, to try and make amends.'

'For someone else's error.'

Her head jerked upwards. 'What does it matter?' Then she regretted her sudden bitterness. 'I'm sorry,

I didn't intend burdening you with it. I'd rather Mother didn't know.'

He paused at the door. 'I appreciate your motives, Jill, even though I don't agree with what you're doing. Have you even begun to consider the consequences if Martin never recovers his memory? You're going to have to live with it for the rest of your life.'

She couldn't answer. The words were too much an echo of what Bruno von Reimer had said. 'I'll manage.' The future was something she no longer even cared to contemplate.

CHAPTER FOUR

IN the next few days, Jill tried to school herself to think of nothing except her work but it was, as she soon discovered, a losing battle because the inevitable hospital gossip revolved solely around the handsome Bruno von Reimer.

He had been gone five days. The gossip didn't go so far as to predict when he would return and the thought hit her with a jolt that perhaps he didn't intend coming back. His fiancée, after all, was in good hands. There was nothing more he could do and he must have other commitments.

Strangely, the idea merely added to her depression and she tried angrily to thrust it away. What did it matter whether he returned or not? Far better if he didn't. Better for herself, the thought crept in to shame her, but what about the girl he loved, who needed him and seemed to draw strength from his presence?

'This is ridiculous,' she told herself. She was even beginning to forget the cardinal rule, that of the welfare of the patient before all else.

'A penny for your thoughts.'

She came to with a start and realised that Helen Cooper was grinning at her from across the table.

'They aren't worth it,' she muttered crossly.

Helen's dark brow rose. 'Are you sure. You were stirring that cup of coffee as if your life depended on it.'

Jill thrust away the spoon and drank the scalding liquid much too quickly. She looked at her watch and rose to her feet. 'If you must know I'm going to see Sister, to see if I can get my old place back on Casualty.'

Helen looked at her askance. 'You don't mean you're going to throw up the chance of seeing the dashing Austrian Baron?'

'Exactly.'

'But you're the envy of the entire hospital.'

'Well the entire hospital can have him,' Jill called as she fled.

Sister received her with considerable impatience. 'No, Nurse, I'm sorry but unless you have some perfectly good reason for your request, a transfer to another ward is quite out of the question.' Her gaze scanned Jill from head to toe. 'Have you a good reason?'

'Yes, Sister, I . . . that is.' How could she explain. It was the best of reasons, she didn't want to have to see that man. Her cheeks coloured as she stared at her hands. 'I preferred my work in Casualty, Sister.'

'Indeed.' Sister's temper suddenly lived up to the colour of her hair. 'Nurse, I think you are wasting my time. Not only would it cause a great deal of inconvenience to have to move you again, I understand that Mr von Reimer has indicated his satisfaction with your work to date and has expressly repeated his request that you remain on this unit.'

Jill stared at the figure behind the desk. 'You mean, he has returned?'

'No, Nurse, I gather Mr von Reimer's plans are still as yet unsettled but he is in regular communication and, naturally, receives reports of his patient's progress.'

'I see.' Jill said woodenly.

Sister rose to her feet and Jill realised that the brief interview was at an end. As she left the small office it seemed that no matter how hard she tried or whatever distance separated her from Bruno von Reimer, he still had the power to reach out and control her life.

She was unaware of anything except a blur of faces as she pushed her way through the swing doors and hurried back to the quiet of the unit where she took over from her relief and automatically began the routine checks. She was glad to see that the patient was sleeping, resting quite easily. In fact there had been a slight but definite improvement during the past twenty-four hours and Jill felt a quick surge of hope.

As she held the thin wrist in order to take her pulse she found herself enviously studying Helga Klammer's perfect complexion and delicate features. Long lashes curled against her cheeks and the generous mouth was relaxed in sleep now that the pain had been alleviated. Her hair lay against the pillow like a golden cloud. She was like the fairy-tale princess waiting for her prince to come along and waken her with a kiss. Except that the very idea of Bruno von Reimer in the role of romantic prince was too ludicrous. He's far more fitted to play the wicked giant ready to lure his innocent victims to his castle, she thought. Then drew herself up sharply. Why was she thinking of him in any role at all?

With leaden hands she filled in the chart before returning it to the clip at the foot of the bed. Beyond the window the sky was dark with the threat of more snow to come. She watched the afternoon visitors gradually beginning to take their leave. The lights were already on, casting shadows and a pale, orange glow across the hospital drive.

Jill moved to switch on the small lamp above the bed and as she did so she saw the girl's lashes flicker. Jill held her breath, then the movement came again and this time they remained open to stare up at her with blurred confusion. She leaned a little closer and smiled.

'Hullo there. How do you feel?'

The girl frowned and licked her dry lips. Jill reached for a glass of water from the locker and supported her as she took a few sips before she lay back against the pillows again. There were shadows of exhaustion beneath her eyes.

'Who are you? Have I seen you before?'

Jill felt a nerve begin to pulse in her throat. 'My name is Jill, Jill Sinclair. I'm a Staff Nurse and I've been looking after you since you came here.' She watched and waited for some reaction but clearly her name had had no impact and, after all, why should it, she thought, reprimanding herself for that near moment of panic. The girl had been brought in unconscious and had been under sedation.

'Where am I?' The blue eyes turned to study the small unit with growing apprehension.

'You're at St Kit's Hospital. But you musn't worry, you're doing very well. The doctors are very pleased with you.'

The blonde head moved restlessly. 'I don't understand.'

'No,' Jill smiled. 'There was an accident, perhaps you don't remember.' She felt the dryness of her mouth as she watched the girl struggling to remember and saw a sudden new sense of panic overwhelm her. What if she did remember, remembered seeing Martin at the wheel of the car?

The blue eyes closed again for a moment then opened, slowly, as she looked at Jill. 'It is all very strange . . . in here.' She pressed a hand against her forehead. Jill noticed her accent was marked and very pleasant. 'Like a picture which is broken, and there are pieces missing. I think . . . there is a car,' the girl said.

Jill felt her stomach tighten. Should she say something, now. Get it over with once and for all. But common sense prevailed. The patient had suffered enough of a shock.

'Yes, there was a car.'

The fact was absorbed in silence for a moment then Helga's brows drew together. 'I was much hurt?'

Jill struggled for an answer. Despite the fact that she had faced situations like this many times since she had qualified, she had never found them becoming easier, nor had she ever before been personally involved.

She was surprised to hear her voice sounding perfectly calm and normal. 'There is some injury to your spine, you may find it will affect your legs.'

The girl stared down at the blankets covering her and her eyes widened with growing terror. 'I do not feel them.' Her voice was very quiet and Jill nodded, taking her hand.

'Sometimes it happens, if the nerves are damaged or badly bruised.' She broke off as tears welled up in the blue eyes. 'The doctors are doing tests and we are still waiting for the results.' She heard the stifled sob.

'You do not have to explain to me. I know how these things are. You are being kind but you are saying nothing because you do not know what to say.'

Jill bit her lip. 'Please, you must try not to worry. It isn't that I won't tell you, we truly haven't had the results yet but the doctor will explain . . .'

'Bruno, where is Bruno? I want to see him.'

'I'm afraid Mr von Reimer had to return to Austria for a few days but we expect him back soon. He is constantly in touch and receives regular reports of your progress.' Her gaze went to the locker. 'He sent those roses.'

Helga turned and Jill saw the look of pleasure flood into her face as she looked at the beautiful, long-stemmed flowers. 'Dear Bruno.' There were tears on her lashes and she frowned again. 'I'm so tired. Stay with me, Nurse, please.'

'Of course I will.' Jill took the out-thrust hand and felt the thin fingers close over her own. 'Go to sleep. I promise I shall be here when you wake up again.'

The lashes were flickering. 'Thank you. If Bruno cannot be here it is good to feel that I have a friend.' And as Jill watched she fell into a proper sleep for the first time.

Slowly Jill released herself and turned blindly from the bed. The girl's touching faith in the man she loved would help her to recover, mentally at least. She knew they had reached a vital turning point. But what of the future? That still remained to be faced and was so insecure. Also, what happened when she learned the truth, or what everyone believed to be the truth, would she still think of Jill then as her friend?

She went about her duties in a daze of wretchedness and had to be reminded to go for lunch by Sister. Not that it was worth the effort of queueing, for although the food was good at St Kits, better in fact than most, she couldn't do justice to steak and kidney pudding and settled for a sandwich. It was against everything they had ever been taught in PTS, the Preliminary Training School. Sister Tutor had stressed over and over again the importance of diet, not only for the patients but themselves. 'Nurses are called upon to do an exacting type of work and it can only be done efficiently, as we expect it to be done at St Kits if the nurse is as diligent in her personal habits as in her studies.' Sister Tutor had been a great advocate, Jill remembered, of early nights and proper meals. But then, Sister Tutor had never suffered the misery of a man like Bruno von Reimer.

Without warning, an image of him leapt into her mind again with such clarity that it left her shaking. 'Pull yourself together,' she told herself angrily. 'You're a fool. He means nothing to you and even if he does he isn't yours and never can be.' But the memory of his kiss wouldn't be thrust away so easily, nor would the feeling that he had been as shaken by the impact of that encounter as she had.

She returned to the Unit, breathing deeply to try and steady her nerves, only to find herself in disgrace with Sister because she was three minutes late and Dr Reynolds wanted to examine the patient.

'I'm sorry, Sister,' Jill whispered in mortified tones. 'I had to queue . . .'

'Never mind that now, Nurse. For heaven's sake just bring the trolley and let me have the notes.' Sister hurried away to stand beside the bed as Dr Reynolds completed the ophthalmic examination of the retina he had been making. It was one of the routine neurological checks to be made, along with blood samples and various tests upon the reflexes.

Jill passed the X-rays and stood silently while they studied them. Her movements were entirely automatic, just as she also moved without thinking to hold the frightened girl's hand as yet another lumbar puncture was performed.

By the time the examinations were finished she lay against the pillows looking pale and exhausted and Jill remained behind as Sister finally bustled away in the wake of Dr Reynolds.

'There.' She carefully rearranged the sheet and set the bedside locker back in its customary position so that the girl could see the roses. 'I'm sorry, I know these things make you feel uncomfortable and depressed, but they have to be done and they will help.'

'Yes, I know. You are very kind and I am glad you were here. But still I should be happier if Bruno would come back.' Her lips trembled then she turned her head away and finally slept.

During the next few days Jill was pleased to note a still further improvement in the girl's progress but, to her dismay, along with it she saw a growing awareness of the concern the doctors felt about the lack of response as far as the spinal injuries went.

Helga's questions were tentative at first and Jill managed to parry them fairly successfully, but for how much longer she wondered. Nor was her own task made any easier by the growing friendship which was springing up between them, and that in itself gave Jill fresh cause for anxiety. It was something she would rather have avoided, reminding herself again and again of the cardinal rule that one didn't become emotionally involved with one's patients yet she found herself drawn to the girl who had, until now, accepted all the pain and frustrations of her condition with admirable bravery. There were a few lapses into depression but they were inevitable and Jill couldn't help contrasting her behaviour with that of Martin. He had taken his injuries so badly yet this girl had far more to lose.

It shocked her to discover that she could have been so poor a judge of character, her own perhaps more than any. She hadn't believed she could be so weak. It had taken Bruno von Reimer to show her the truth about herself and she didn't like what she saw.

She straightened the bed cover then turned to remove a wilted flower from the vase on the locker. 'They were beautiful while they lasted, weren't they?' she said. 'But I'm afraid in this heat they don't stand much of a chance.'

'I feel like the flowers also. Everyone is very kind but I feel closed in.'

'Yes, I'm sorry. I know it's difficult for you.

71

Perhaps very soon we can arrange to have you moved into one of the side wards.'

'You think that is possible?' Helga's blue eyes widened hopefully.

'Well, I can't make any promises you understand. The decision will be up to the doctor. But if you go on at this rate, well I don't see why not. The room isn't much bigger I'm afraid, but at least you'll be able to see and hear a little more of what goes on.'

'I should like that.'

Jill smiled. 'It's a nice day.' She stood at the window. 'It's actually stopped snowing and the sun is shining at last.' She was making a conscious effort to cheer the girl up but as she turned she saw the sudden restlessness in the pale features.

'I love the snow. At home we ski all the time . . .'

'And you will again.' A sudden idea struck her. 'Look, why don't I move your bed just a little and arrange this mirror so that you can see outside?' She drew the curtains back as far as they would go and gently manoeuvred the bed. 'There, is that better?'

'You are very kind.'

'Nonsense. It's my job.'

'Even so,' Helga studied her gravely, 'to some a job is just that, they bring to it no humanity. But you . . . I am glad I have you to care for me. I am grateful to Bruno for choosing you.'

Jill swallowed hard. Gratitude was the last thing she deserved or wanted. Perhaps this was the time to tell her the truth as everyone believed it, that she was to blame for the accident, before their friendship developed too far. It would come as less of a shock and far, far better than to have her learn of it from Bruno von Reimer.

It was as if a cold hand had clasped at her heart. Why should she care what he thought of her, she chided herself for the hundredth time. But the fact was that she did care and it hurt deeply, the injustice of it. Not that it could make any difference to their relationship but if only he would not think so ill of her, that at least would be more bearable than his contempt.

She drew in a deep breath and looked down at the girl in the bed. 'As a matter of fact there is something you should know.' In the mirror she caught a glimpse of her own face and was shocked to see the pinched, drawn look. Was he really capable of having such an effect upon her? If so then the sooner she explained and was free of him the better. 'It is true that Mr von Reimer arranged for me to special you . . .'

'Ah, then there you are.' Helga was smiling. 'He is very wise. He wanted us to become friends.'

Jill's mouth was dry. How far from the truth that was, but how could she tell this trusting girl that her fiancée was capable of such calculated cruelty.

'You must love him very much.' The words almost stuck in her throat.

'Oh yes, for a long time. I could not imagine my life without him. But you know how he is.'

Jill's lips were stiff from smiling. 'Yes, I do.' Mechanically she put out the dosage of tablets prescribed and carried them towards the bed.

'Helga . . . I, look there is something I must tell you.' She brushed a hand against her brow. 'It isn't easy but you have a right to know.' She wished she could avoid the trusting look in the blue eyes but it wasn't possible. 'It is to do with the accident. You see . . .'

'I think that will do, Nurse.'

She spun round, the colour draining from her face as the voice came from behind her. Dimly she was aware of the cry of delight from Helga, saw her outstretched hands but it was the figure framed in the doorway which held her, his features implacable yet a warning smile played about his mouth as he looked at her.

How long had he been standing there? How much had he heard? Obviously enough to guess her intentions but then why had he stopped her. Her knees felt strangely weak and she realised bitterly that perhaps that was a privilege he was reserving for himself, when it suited *his* purpose.

She knew she was staring at him and the sight of his tall, masculine ruggedness left her feeling ridiculously shaken. She drew herself up. It was useless to go on like this. Her gaze fell before the piercing stare but she refused to be thwarted.

'I have decided to explain,' her voice challenged and faltered as he moved closer, so close that she could almost feel the nearness of him. She clasped her hands against her apron unaware of the haunted expression in her eyes. She was too tired to fight him any more but, as always, it seemed he must take the advantage from her, stripping away her defences.

He regarded her coolly. 'I would recommend that you consider very seriously before taking any such step, Nurse.' He spoke quietly but the words were like a drill, penetrating her numbed brain. 'Your first duty is to your patient, and I have no wish that she be upset, is that perfectly clear?'

She ground her teeth together. He spoke so softly that their conversation couldn't be overheard yet it was as if he was ensnaring her in a trap and however she fought she couldn't escape.

'I said is that clear, Nurse?'

Her eyes filled with tears. He was right, but that only made things worse. His fiancée was still very weak in spite of the improvement and there was no way of knowing how she might react to a confession of guilt. She should have taken all this into consideration.

Jill glared at him, her mouth quivering and her eyes blazing. 'Yes, Herr Doktor, perfectly clear.' She saw the brief look of mocking triumph before she turned and sped from the room and her last glimpse was of him walking quickly towards Helga's eagerly outstretched arms.

CHAPTER FIVE

JILL had completed the writing of her report. She looked ruefully at the handwriting which was lacking its customary neatness but at least it was concise and in that respect Sister would have no cause for complaint.

Her head was throbbing and she decided to go across to her room in the Nurses' Home, take a couple of aspirins, have a bath and an early night. Not that she expected to sleep but at least she could be alone with her misery.

She collected her cape and was hurrying towards the swing doors when Keith Hammond saw her. He was talking to one of his colleagues and she almost hoped he would let her pass by uninterrupted but not so. With a smile he excused himself and came over to her, matching his steps to her own.

'Hi, I'm glad I caught you.'

With an effort she managed to stifle a yawn. She liked the tall Australian and knew that the feeling had been mutual ever since his arrival at St Kits when they had first met at a hospital dance. They had shared several dates, going for a meal or to the local cinema, attending the various hospital functions together until the grapevine had inevitably had them engaged and practically married. In fact Keith

76

had proposed, twice, but on both occasions Jill had found herself holding back, jokingly discouraging in a way which wouldn't hurt. She liked him very much but that didn't mean she felt ready for marriage and liking didn't seem to be sufficient grounds for committing herself to something as important as sharing her life with another person.

She responded half-heartedly to his greeting and was then ashamed. She felt not only physically but mentally exhausted and the last thing she wanted was to get involved in a conversation.

'I don't see much of you these days,' he said. 'Where are you hiding yourself?'

She managed to smile. 'I'm not hiding, Keith. You know I was taken off Casualty and moved up to the special unit to keep an eye on Mr von Reimer's patient.'

'Oh yes, sure.' His face clouded momentarily. 'Giving you a hard time is he?'

She shook her head, burying her hands determinedly in her pockets. 'No, not really. I'm just tired that's all. How's Casualty?'

'Same as always. Like a cauldron for ever on the boil.'

'I know what you mean. I miss it, strangely enough.'

'Oh well, I suppose there's no accounting for taste.'

In spite of herself she laughed. 'You know what I mean. Always something different happening, new faces, no time to think.'

He paused, holding the swing doors for her. 'You don't want to let it get you down, you know. I mean, why anticipate the worst? There's a good chance the kid may walk again.'

His astute reading of her thoughts brought her up sharply. Was it so obvious? Was she carrying her guilt ... Martin's guilt around with her so openly? She walked ahead of him and shivered as a blast of cold air met her. 'Only an even chance. That's not such good odds when you're twenty years old and engaged to be married, is it?' Her gaze flickered up and fell again as his hand closed gently over her arm.

'It's not like you to take it so much to heart.'

'I was never involved, not personally, before.' She said drily. 'This is rather different you know, Keith.'

'Of course it is. I didn't mean to sound callous.'

'No.' Her hand closed quickly over his. 'I know you didn't. And I didn't mean to snap. It's just that I've had one hell of a day and I'm tired. I don't know why but it's as if that wretched man von Reimer has put some sort of jinx on me. I even got a ticking off from Sister the other day for being late back on duty. It was just one of those things. I was late getting away for lunch, then I had to queue ... By the time I eventually got back, Dr Reynolds had already begun examining the patient and Sister's temper wasn't improved. Oh, you know how it is.'

He studied her closely. 'I know you're taking the whole thing much too seriously. Okay, you were late but it's not the end of the world. You're not likely to make a habit of it and Sister knows you well enough to realise that. Look,' his grin broke through, 'what you need is to get away from here for a couple of hours, a change of scene.'

Her heart sank as she anticipated what was coming and hurried on down the corridor. 'No, Keith. I'm tired. I'm going to have an early night.'

He moved in front of her so that she had to stop. 'Are you sure it's an early night you need, Jill, or are you running away?'

Her eyes widened. 'I don't know what you mean.'

'Oh, I think you do. The question is, is it me or von Reimer or both, and why?'

She couldn't trust herself to speak. She felt his arm go round her shoulders but made no protest. It was good to be held in his arms, to feel protected, safe. Suddenly she felt the tears pricking at her eyes. But she musn't break down here, not where everyone could see.

'Look, why don't we go somewhere quiet,' Keith was saying persuasively. 'That Italian restaurant. You always liked that.'

Yes she did, and suddenly the burden of misery, the thought of going back to her lonely room and lying awake for hours was too much to bear.

'I won't be very good company,' she warned, and he grinned.

'In that case I'll have to be cheerful enough for the two of us.'

'Oh Keith, really, you're incorrigible.' She laughed and he was pleased. 'You'll have to wait

79

while I change into something a bit more appropriate.'

'That's okay. Tell you what, I'll wait for you in reception. Half an hour?'

She gave in without any real regret. Perhaps he was right, that what she needed was to get away rather than sit around moping. After all, why should she give Bruno von Reimer yet another victory, that of knowing that he could make her life miserable? At least away from the hospital she wasn't likely to run the risk of falling over him for a few hours.

'Fine.' She hurried away and was surprised to find herself even beginning to look forward to it.

She had a quick shower, brushed her hair and slipped on a soft, blue dress with a high collar and a full skirt which emphasised the slenderness of her waist. She slipped her feet into a pair of blue, strappy sandals, totally impractical but what did that matter? Tonight she was not a nurse, she was Jill Sinclair. Even so, looking in the mirror at her reflection she was startled to see how different she looked out of uniform and the knowledge, or perhaps the shedding of the starched white apron and dress, seemed to give her an added confidence. This was someone Bruno von Reimer couldn't reach. But as she ran down the stairs to meet Keith she felt ridiculously as if she was running to escape the wicked giant who meant to hold her prisoner.

The meal was good, as always, and Luigi had made them welcome, commenting upon their too long absence. He had bustled them to a table in a secluded alcove where the light was subdued and as they ate their food and drank their wine in the relaxed atmosphere, Jill gradually began to feel her tensions melt away. She wasn't even really aware of the other diners who came and went.

'I like it here,' she smiled, savouring the heady wine.

'So do I, when I'm with you.' Keith's hand reached out to touch hers as her fingers curled round the stem of her glass.

Involuntarily she frowned. 'Please, Keith, don't, don't spoil it.' Her eyes lifted imploringly to his but for once he chose to ignore the appeal.

'I'm sorry, Jill, but you must know how I feel about you and I've always hoped you might feel the same about me.'

She bit her lip. 'I'm very fond of you, you know that.'

'Well then, why don't you say you'll marry me.' He grinned. 'Surely I'm not such an ugly guy?'

In spite of herself she laughed, her hand tightening over his. 'No, of course you're not.' Quite the contrary, she thought. He was handsome and a man most of her friends would envy her. Marriage to Keith would mean security and he would never do anything to hurt her she knew. Perhaps she was looking for too much, some kind of excitement which didn't actually exist, was just a myth. The kind of excitement which would come from loving a man like Bruno von Reimer. She set her glass down quickly, almost too quickly, spilling some of her wine. Now why had she thought such a thing? She was glad of the subdued lighting which hid the sudden flush of her cheeks. 'It wouldn't be fair to you Keith if I were to say yes when I'm still so unsure. What kind of wife would that make me?'

'The kind of wife I want, Jill.'

'But liking isn't enough grounds for marriage. You deserve better.'

'You can't get better than the best there is. I love you, Jill.' His gaze looked earnestly into hers and she had to struggle with the sudden lump in her throat. She knew she would be a fool not to say yes. She could make him a good wife. She would work at it, he wouldn't ever have cause to regret it.

She was conscious of someone brushing past the table and pausing to pick up her napkin which had fallen to the floor. It was dropped on to the table in front of her but the figure made no move to leave.

'Good evening, Nurse Sinclair, Hammond. I trust you enjoyed your meal?'

Her gaze flew up and she felt her heart contract painfully as she stared up into the mocking features of Bruno von Reimer. Oh no, it couldn't be, not here. She knew her anger was unjustified but somehow that didn't lessen it. He was like a shadow, haunting her wherever she went. 'It must be nice to escape one's duties so easily for a while.'

The barb was so clearly aimed at herself that she gasped at the injustice of it. Her fingers tightened round her glass but somehow she managed to force herself to smile. 'Yes, Herr von Reimer, it is. The pity is that we must return to them.'

'Ah.' The mocking gaze lingered with such intensity that she felt the colour drain from her face. 'But then few of us have a choice, Nurse.' He bowed his head and was gone before she could frame a further reply. She was surprised to find that she was shaking as she watched him being led to a secluded table and suddenly all her former tiredness returned, leaving her drained and miserable. But at least Keith didn't seem to have noticed anything amiss.

'Strange chap that,' he murmured. 'Brilliant of course, I mean, how many men of his age can combine a career in neurology and surgery?'

Jill gathered up her bag with fingers which seemed numb. 'Look, I'm sorry, Keith, but do you mind if we go. I've really got quite a headache and we've both got an early start in the morning. If I don't get some sleep I'll be in Sister's bad books again.'

He turned to her, full of concern but at the same time she was aware of the resolve in his eyes. 'Okay, Jill, but don't think I intend letting you get out of giving me an answer so easily, because I don't.'

He paid the bill and as they made their way out she had to resist the urge to turn and see if they were being watched. Then, as they reached the door she saw the table where Bruno von Reimer sat reflected in the glass. He had his back to them and was busy giving his order. Well, I hope it chokes him, she thought. It's what he deserves for having spoilt my evening.

As they drove back to the hospital in virtual silence her brain was in turmoil. She had so nearly said 'yes' to Keith and yet she knew now that to have done so would not only have been a mistake it would have been an act of cruelty which she had no right to inflict. She would never love him as he had a right to expect of the woman he married, but why she should suddenly be so certain of it was something she didn't understand.

She stared unseeingly out of the car window until they reached the hospital where she said a hasty goodnight to Keith before speeding to her room and giving way at last to the flood of tears.

Jill made her way reluctantly to the Unit next day to take over. It was normally her morning off, which usually meant enjoying the luxury of an extra half an hour's lie-in before doing all the tasks which had been neglected during the week, such as washing her hair, sorting out laundry, writing letters. But she realised that to have a morning off today would only have encouraged her to think and to lie awake worrying for most of the night, without finding any solutions.

Eventually, pale and weary-eyed she had got up and gone for a long walk, only to find that she had walked so far that she was almost late getting back and had to rush to change into her uniform.

She centred her anger resentfully upon Bruno von Reimer. If only he had never come into her life. Everything had been so peaceful, so well ordered, until he had come on the scene. Angrily she fastened the belt round her neat waist and secured her cap over her hair staring at her reflection in the mirror. 'Well, I suppose it can't go on for ever,' she told herself, without much conviction. Helga Klammer was making progress and presumably, sooner or later, would return home.

St Kits was enjoying one of its quiet afternoons. Visitors were at liberty to come and go at most reasonable times during the day but visiting time was officially in the evening, which made it easier for most working people.

Jill entered the Unit, pausing for a moment to check that her cap was straight, and as she did so she heard Bruno von Reimer's voice. The door was cracked open. She knew she should go in but was incapable of movement and, as she stood there, Helga's voice came to her, tearfully.

'But I have so much time, lying here, to think about it and I believe the wedding should be post-poned if not cancelled altogether.'

There was a silence before Jill heard him say with incredible gentleness, 'Nonsense, Helga. I see no reason to put it off. You're making a good recovery.'

There was a stifled sob. 'You tell me I am but how can you be sure? What if I never walk again?'

Jill pressed a hand to her mouth as he spoke, more firmly. 'Why don't you trust me? There is every reason to hope.'

'I do, I do trust you, but still I am lying here and it would be so unfair to marry like this . . .'

'It would be even more unfair to deny the man who loves you so deeply, my dear.'

Somehow Jill managed to frame her features into a mask as she moved towards the door. She had to unclench her hands in order to push it open.

'Good afternoon, sir.' She entered briskly as if she had heard nothing of their conversation but her eyes took in the girl's flushed cheeks and the tear-filled eyes. Purposely she avoided looking at Bruno von Reimer yet she was conscious of his gaze, coolly following her, undoubtedly comparing her appearance now with that of last night. She wanted to turn and run but that, of course, was impossible. Instead she turned to challenge him only to falter again as he said coldly:

'Did you enjoy your evening out, Nurse?'

Her hand trembled as she reached for the chart from the foot of the bed. 'Yes, thank you, sir.'

He had risen to his feet and it was as if his presence immediately filled the room.

'I wasn't aware that you knew Dr Hammond in anything other than a professional capacity.'

She drew in a breath. Surely he didn't intend questioning her about her private life now? Her chin rose. 'As a matter of fact Keith and I are very good friends but then, there is absolutely no reason why you should know, is there, sir? After all, what I do in my off duty time is entirely my own affair.'

The dark eyes narrowed and she knew that he was mocking her. 'Entirely your own affair, Nurse. But I noticed that you and your . . . friend left rather early. I merely hoped that my arrival didn't drive you away. That particular restaurant is one of my favourites.'

'Not at all.' She regarded him with a coolness she was far from feeling. 'I was tired. I'd been on duty all day and had a headache.'

'I'm sorry to hear that, Nurse. You do look very pale. Are you sure you're well?'

'Perfectly, thank you.' She clamped her lips tightly. This sudden concern for her was out of character. Was he daring to imply that one evening out affected her efficiency?

To her dismay she dropped the clip-board and it clattered to the floor at her feet. He bent quickly to retrieve it but made no attempt to relinquish it as she reached for it. For a moment their eyes met and a tremor ran through her.

'I would like to speak to you for a moment, Nurse, outside.' His hand was on her arm.

'But my patient . . .'

'Is asleep again and will be perfectly safe for a few moments.' His grip tightened as Jill cast an anxious glance towards the bed and she knew he was giving her no choice. With an arrogance she had come to accept as typical of him he drew her outside the door.

'You're hurting my arm,' she protested and, as if only then realising that he had kept his hold of her, he released her abruptly.

'I was afraid you might try to escape me, Nurse.'

She drew in her breath sharply. 'It wouldn't do

me much good, would it?' And to her chagrin she saw him smile.

'None at all. I'm glad you've begun to realise that at last.'

Jill's cheeks had flushed a dull scarlet. Would he never cease to punish her? Her eyes filled with angry tears. 'I hate you. Why can't you leave me alone?' Even as she spoke she was filled with a sense of remorse. His face was drawn, his mouth a narrow line as he moved closer. Surely he must be able to hear the hammering of her heart?

'Do you, Nurse?' he said softly. 'Do you really.'

Her breath caught in her throat and only by a supreme effort did she find the strength to draw away.

'Yes, I do.'

He straightened up and his expression became suddenly colder.

'Well, that's a pity because we shall be seeing a lot more of each other in the future.'

Her heart beat faster as a sudden premonition began to envelop her.

'Wh . . . what do you mean?'

If he heard the question he chose to ignore it. 'Tell me, Nurse, just what is the relationship between yourself and Dr Hammond?'

The blatant impertinence of the question took her so completely by surprise that she was caught off-guard. For a moment she stared at him. Surely he wasn't serious? But one look at his face told her that this was no idle curiosity.

'I fail to see that my relationship with Dr Hammond is any concern of yours,' she snapped.

His brows drew together. 'On the contrary, Nurse, I am making it my concern.'

'But you have no right . . .'

'I think I have.' He spoke softly yet she sensed the hint of a threat behind the words.

Her chin rose. She would show him that she wouldn't be intimidated. 'If you must know, Dr Hammond has asked me to marry him.'

'I see. And your answer?'

She floundered, for some reason unable to bring out a lie. 'I . . . I haven't given him any answer yet.'

'I'm pleased to hear it because it would be a pity to have to tell him that you've changed your mind, wouldn't it?'

She gasped. 'What do you mean, changed my mind. Why should I do any such thing?'

'Oh, for one very good reason, Nurse. You see I'm not satisfied with Miss Klammer's progress and I've decided to move her to my private clinic in Austria.'

'But . . . surely, the risks . . .' she stammered. 'Isn't this decision rather sudden?'

'Yes it is, and I'm well aware of the risks, Nurse, but I think we have reached a stage in her treatment when she will do better in surroundings she knows and where I shall have the time and facilities I need to help her recover.'

Jill's mouth felt dry. He was watching her closely. 'And just what has this to do with me?'

'It's quite simple, Nurse, I've decided you will come with me in order to continue the nursing care.' He went on as if completely unaware of the effect his words were having, of the sudden whiteness of her face. 'Of course, there's no way of knowing how long it will be needed, but everything has been taken care of. I've made all the arrangements, that was the reason for my recent return to Austria. You'll leave with us next week. You'll see now, of course, why I'm glad you hadn't committed yourself to Dr Hammond. It would have been most inconvenient.'

Her mouth opened but no words came. She couldn't believe any of this was happening. Gradually anger asserted itself as she faced him. 'You mean that you actually went ahead and made the arrangements. Just like that, without even consulting me?' Her voice shook. 'How dare you. Didn't it even occur to you that I might refuse?'

'Dare?' he said coldly. 'I didn't see any need to consult you, Nurse. And as for your refusing, I hardly think that's likely, after all you have some responsibility towards the patient and I don't intend that you should forget it quite so easily.'

She felt faint. He was trapping her yet again and, what was worse, he almost seemed to enjoy seeing her struggle.

'But . . . I can't possibly go.' Her voice was little more than a whisper.

'As I said, Nurse, the arrangements are made.' In the artificial light her face was pale and her eyes wide as she stared at him. He frowned. 'There is of course another reason why I think you will not refuse.'

Her head jerked up. She still couldn't speak.

'Your brother. I make no promises,' he added quickly. 'I shall need to make further examinations but there may be some treatment. At least I am willing to try. The question is, are you?'

She licked her lips. 'You mean . . . he may be able to play again?'

'I have said, no promises. *If* I operate there may be a possibility.'

'I see,' she said dully. Part of her mind wanted to say 'no' but the rest of her knew that she had no real choice. 'And you will undertake this treatment provided I agree to your terms.'

He shrugged. 'It seems little to ask, Nurse, but perhaps I was mistaken in thinking that you care for your brother or his future, or indeed anything but yourself.'

She shuddered. For one moment she considered calling his bluff by refusing. But then, could she be sure that that was what it was. Could she afford to refuse any chance for Martin? She had the feeling that Bruno von Reimer was aware of her thoughts and she hated him for his arrogance even as she admitted to herself that there was really no question to be answered.

'Very well,' she heard herself say. 'I will do it.' She almost imagined she heard him give a slight intake of breath as if of relief but that was ridiculous of course and his gaze, when she could bring herself to look at him, was impassive as ever. How could she ever imagine him capable of any stirrings of conscience.

'I'm glad,' he said simply. 'You've made a wise decision. Helga will be pleased, she has taken a fondness to you and anything which makes her happy must enhance her chances of a proper recovery.'

The irony of his words sickened Jill. 'I must get back to my patient.'

'Yes, of course.' Having won he made no further attempt to hold her and she heard him take his leave without seeing him go. It was as much as she could do to keep her mind on her work afterwards. Next week, he had said. So soon. It was scarcely enough time to make her own arrangements. At least her passport was in order and so was Martin's. Almost against her will she felt the vague tremor of excitement and then another thought came to dull it. If she was to work at the clinic, she would also have to witness his marriage to Helga.

The rest of the week was like a bad dream, except that one woke up from dreams whereas there seemed no end to this.

CHAPTER SIX

WHATEVER her opinion of Bruno von Reimer she certainly couldn't fault his arrangements for removal of the patients. Everything, from the journey to the airport by ambulance, the flight itself and the journey which actually brought them to the clinic had been masterminded to the very last detail. Not that she should have expected otherwise, Jill told herself. Everything he undertook received the same meticulous attention to detail. Even so, by the time they reached the clinic, Helga was showing obvious signs of distress and Jill sped to help get her settled into the waiting bed before she had time even to consider her own exhaustion.

She felt less concern for Martin's physical state. He had stood the flight well, enjoyed it even, despite the fact that he too, was obviously tired. But, on arrival he was led away to his own room by one of the nurses and seemed quite happy to relinquish himself into the care of strangers. It was his mental attitude that worried her most. She had imagined he would be overjoyed when she gave him the news about the possibility of an operation, carefully leaving out her own part of the bargain. But he had received it instead with a surliness which had filled her with dread.

'This chap Reimer may be good,' he had told her bitterly, 'but I'll believe in miracles when I actually sit at a piano and play a piece of Chopin again.'

'He doesn't make any promises, you realise that?' she had said, warily, and he had leaned his head back and closed his eyes.

'If he can't give me any guarantee then I'd rather he left me alone.'

'But you surely can't mean that?' she protested. 'Martin, you have to give this a try.'

'Why?' He had retaliated with a bitterness which stung. 'What do you know about it. It's my life. I'll decide what risks to take with what's left of it.'

He was being deliberately cruel yet she sensed that it wasn't aimed directly at herself so much as at his own helplessness, as if he could hide behind a barrier where nothing more could hurt him.

Feeling thoroughly dispirited she had left him. During the flight she had remained close to Helga while Martin had occupied the seat next to Bruno von Reimer, thus they had exchanged few words. 'Perhaps it was as well,' she thought, staring out of the window onto a layer of thick, curling cloud. 'I only seem to be holding him back.'

Once or twice she saw the two men locked deep in conversation and wondered what it was they discussed. She even saw Martin smile and had to admit ruefully to herself that even in that direction Bruno von Reimer had had more success than herself.

The actual journey from the airport out to the clinic all passed in something of a blur to Jill. It was dark by the time her patient was lifted safely aboard a waiting ambulance and the air was bitingly cold. She gazed out of the window at the snow as they climbed steadily along narrow roads to the mountain village where she had been told the clinic was situated. Occasionally she saw lights flickering in the distance. The attendant travelling with them told her that some were from the chair-lift points which carried skiers up to the high slopes.

Finally they were there. Jill climbed out, feeling her boots crunch in the snow as she stood waiting while the stretcher was lifted down. She followed up the steps as they all hurried inside, and then came the task of ensuring that the patient had suffered no ill effects from the journey and of settling her down for the night. Only when all was finally finished did Jill realise just how exhausted she was.

'You go now.' The pretty young nurse who had greeted them upon arrival smiled at Jill. 'It has been a long day for you too. We can take over.'

Jill eased her aching back. She had taken an instant liking to the blonde-haired girl whose quiet efficiency had impressed itself upon her at once so that she felt no qualms about relinquishing her charge. Even so, her glance darted towards Bruno von Reimer who, for once, seemed scarcely aware of her presence. It was strange to see him on his home ground and taking control so easily.

He turned, frowning briefly in her direction. 'Yes, by all means, Nurse. There's nothing more you can do here. Get some rest. You've earned it.'

95

Surprise at the few words of faint praise flickered in Jill's eyes, then she saw the lines of weariness etched into his own face and wondered if he would take his own advice. Somehow she doubted it and, sure enough, as she left she saw him already bent over the girl in the bed, gently making the necessary checks and examination.

'I will show you to your room.' A dark-haired young girl led the way. 'The clinic is not large but it is easy enough to become lost if you don't know it.' She smiled. 'I am Lisel.'

'And I'm Jill.' She stifled a yawn. 'I'm afraid it will take some time to remember everyone's names. The nurse I left with Miss Klammer . . .'

'Ah, yes, that is Krista. She has been here for five years now. She came from one of the big hospitals in Innsbruck at the personal request of the Herr Doktor.' She paused and held open a door. 'Here is your room. It is small but you will find it comfortable I think.'

Jill stepped inside and looked around her with immediate pleasure. Small it may be but it was fresh and airy. The bed quilt matched the curtains and there was a bright rug on the floor in front of a small desk and chair.

'It's perfect.' She smiled. 'A far cry from the Nurses' Home at St Kits.'

'We are very informal here at the clinic, as you will soon see.' Lisel crossed to draw the curtains and switch on a small lamp. Her face darkened. 'It is a pity about Miss Klammer, but she will soon be well now that she is in her own country again and has the Herr Doktor to care for her.'

'I hope you're right.' Jill said earnestly, wondering just how much the staff here knew of the circumstances surrounding the accident. Oh well, no doubt sooner or later she would find out.

Left to her own devices she began to unpack. It had been a hurried business, gathering together sufficient clothes to bring with her and she realised now that the things she had brought were hardly going to be appropriate for the climate. It was something she would have to remedy as soon as possible. There hadn't been time before the flight.

She was delighted to find that her room opened onto a small balcony and she stepped out, for the first time conscious of breathing in the clean, fresh air. She could see nothing beyond the few distant lights but there was an atmosphere which hit her, nothing tangible, which had something to do with the silence through which every sound seemed to echo.

A few flakes of snow were beginning to fall. Jill shivered and stepped back into her room, deciding to have a quick shower and an early night. Lisel had said there would be a meal waiting for her in the dining room but Jill decided to give it a miss. She had no appetite and anyway, under the circumstances no one would be likely to be surprised by her absence. Tomorrow would be time enough to begin to establish a routine, she thought, as she climbed wearily into bed at last.

She woke early the following morning and it was some moments before she could remember where she was. Then, with the realisation, came a feeling of depression. It was dispelled to some degree however by the view which greeted her as she stepped out onto her balcony and gasped with pleasure at the view before her.

The clinic, she saw now, was set upon a slope and from her room she looked out across a valley in which a small village nestled. Everything was snow-covered. Even the trees looked as if they had been decorated with silver and white as the early morning sun glinted on the ice. She drew in her breath as her gaze rose to the mountains which dominated everything, casting giant shadows at this moment over the village below.

It was only with difficulty that she managed to tear herself away, reminding herself as she dressed that she was here, not as a tourist, but to work. Even so, she promised herself a walk down to the village as soon as possible, always assuming of course that she was given the opportunity. But surely even Bruno von Reimer couldn't keep her here twenty-four hours out of every day without a break?

Thoughts of him somehow added momentum to her actions and she dressed quickly in her uniform. Looking at her appearance in the mirror now she was struck suddenly by the formality of it in comparison with that of the staff she had seen last night. She had been surprised to see that no one wore the starched apron and belt but simply light, pastel shade overalls of varying colours according, she presumed, to rank. It had looked very attractive.

She made her way downstairs to breakfast and had hot rolls and coffee in the attractive dining room from which, seated at a table by the window, she could look out across the snow-covered slopes.

She was joined, to her delight, by Krista and it wasn't long before she discovered the truth of the statement that life at the clinic was as informal as circumstances permitted it to be.

'I think it's time I presented myself at Dr von Reimer's office so that I can discover exactly what my duties are to be,' she said.

'Oh but, the Herr Doktor is already making his rounds.'

'Oh no'. Jill groaned and the other girl smiled.

'Do not worry. He knows that you are not yet aware of our ways and he will see you later. In the meantime I am to show you round. It is his wish that you make yourself as much at home as possible.'

Jill finished her coffee and set the cup down, a trifle angrily. 'Even so, I wish I'd realised. I would have arranged for someone to give me a call.' The very idea of starting off on the wrong foot left her with a feeling of unease which was not entirely banished by the girl's gentle reassurance.

'But you must not concern yourself. It was the Herr Doktor himself who gave the order that you were to rest.'

'How very considerate of him and how very out of character.' Jill murmured drily, 'But I expect no favours. As soon as I know my way around I wish to begin work.'

'Then I will show you.' Krista smiled. 'He said he thought it might be so. Come, I will take you to him as soon as we have made a tour of the clinic and you begin to find your bearings.'

Jill followed, her cheeks burning. So he had anticipated her response. Well that was all to the good. At least he would realise that she meant to stick to her side of the bargain and he must keep to his.

Seen in daylight Jill realised that her impression of last night had been a false one for in fact the clinic was larger than she had imagined. They walked along bright, airy corridors and made their way upstairs to the third storey where, as on all the others, each ward had its own balcony where beds could be wheeled out when the weather permitted.

'We are lucky,' Krista said, 'and our patients more so. Many of them come to us with respiratory ailments. Even in this day and age tuberculosis is still with us but it is no longer a sentence of death as it might once have been. You see . . .' She led the way into a ward which held ten beds, 'We encourage those patients who are able to walk, to sit out there when it is not too cold. Apart from the fresh air which helps their recovery it gives them also a sense of freedom and that too, can be very important to someone who is confined to hospital for many weeks.'

'I know exactly what you mean,' Jill nodded approvingly, remembering St Kit's ancient and crumbling façade which, despite all attempts at brightening the wards with colourful curtains and bedspreads, did nothing to hide the fact that the hospital was not only a victim of age but of pollution. 'They are lucky to be able to come to a place like this.'

'Indeed, but also fortunate to have a man such as Dr von Reimer to care for them, a man who is not only brilliant but dedicated.'

'You make him sound like a god.'

'To us he is, or as near as any human being can come to it,' the girl replied, quietly. 'He has saved many lives and it is not only the private cases, there are many who can afford to pay nothing but he never turns them away.'

Jill had the uncomfortable sensation of being brought face to face with a stranger and the image was one she found hard to reconcile with her own experience of the man. She made no comment however as she was led along the corridor to more wards and treatment rooms. Everywhere she saw equipment as modern and sophisticated as any back at home and even some which St Kits would have been proud to boast.

'We also have our own operating theatre,' Krista said.

'What about staff?' Jill peered through the glass doors.

'We have two other resident doctors on call. Apart from that we have thirty nurses. We are a small clinic but the Herr Doktor prefers it so. In this way one can keep a much more personal contact with the patients.'

'I notice you also use Christian names.'

'This too is to put patients at ease and we find it also helps to make a happy atmosphere for staff. I will show you now to your brother's room if you wish.'

They entered a small four-bedded ward though, at that moment, only two were occupied. Martin seemed comfortable enough and Jill was glad to see that he was even taking an interest in his surroundings.

Krista smiled. 'Perhaps you would care to take a walk in the grounds of the clinic, Herr Sinclair?'

Jill saw the look of surprise which deepened into pleasure as he looked at the nurse. 'Is that possible, I mean, is it allowed?'

Her laughter rang out pleasantly. 'But of course. Indeed it is encouraged in patients who are not confined to bed.' Crossing to the window she pushed it open sending a shower of powder-fine snow falling from the sill. 'For the moment it is best you do not go too far. There are still examinations to be made and we would not wish that you tire yourself. But there is a walk which many of our patients take when the weather is good. You can see it from here. This road leads from the clinic through a small wood and back through our gardens.'

'And the other?' Martin was beside her now.

'That goes to the village and on from there again a short distance into Seefeld where there will be many tourists who come for the skiing and skating, or just to sit and admire our scenery.'

His gaze turned from the window to her face and he smiled. 'Well, I can't say I blame them for that. Perhaps I'll take up your idea.'

'Good. But it is best you wait first until the Herr Doktor has made his examination.'

Standing quietly at the door Jill saw his pleasure fade to be replaced by the familiar sullenness.

'And just when will that be, for all the good it will do.'

If Krista noticed the bitterness in his voice she ignored it, answering with a cheerfulness which Jill admired. 'That I cannot say precisely, but very soon I am sure. The Doktor is a very busy man. He wastes no time.'

'Well, I'm glad to hear it because I don't fancy spending the rest of my life sitting here, waiting.'

'Martin!' Jill intervened sharply, more sharply than she had intended. 'For heaven's sake, give it a chance and can't you try to be at least a little gracious? You don't know how lucky you are to be here . . .'

His narrowed gaze studied her. 'And just why am I here, tell me that? A special favour was it? Did you sweet talk him into it just to ease your own conscience?'

She gasped with shock and it subsided leaving her shaking with anger. Clamping her teeth on a reply, she turned and fled before she could say something she would regret, leaving Krista to stare after her, confusion written all over her pretty face. When the girl joined her moments later Jill was leaning against the balcony, her head bent as she forced back the tears.

She started as the girl spoke behind her, her face full of concern.

'Please, you must not take his words to heart. He is afraid and spoke hastily. It happens. I have seen it many times but already he regrets it.'

Jill drew herself up. 'Does he? Somehow I doubt that.' Her eyes searched the other girl's face and she drew a deep breath, 'I suppose you may as well know . . . Martin was a musician, a pianist. Very good too. He had just been offered a scholarship but there was an accident . . .'

'Yes.' To her surprise the girl intervened sadly. 'I have heard this and it is a terrible burden for you to bear.'

Jill stared, dismayed. 'You . . . you know?'

'But yes.' Krista frowned. 'The Herr Doktor explained the circumstances when he came over to make the arrangements. Not to all the staff you understand, just to those who would be involved with your brother's treatment.'

'I see.' Jill gritted her teeth. So he had wasted no time in seeing to it that her position here would be made as untennable as possible.

'Please,' Krista said, 'do not misunderstand . . .'

'Oh, I don't. On the contrary I understand perfectly,' Jill said bleakly. 'And now, if you don't mind, I think it's time I presented myself to the office before he finds reason to complain that I am neglecting my duties.'

'He would not do so.' The pretty face relaxed. 'But come, I will take you to him now.'

They turned into a small annexe and at one of the doors Krista paused. 'This is the Herr Doktor's office. The rest is his personal suite.'

'You mean he lives here, at the clinic? But I understood that his family were very wealthy.'

'That is so. But he chooses to be here, where he is needed.'

'I see.' Jill said lamely. Her brain was in turmoil. How was it possible that one man could have such different sides to his character and why had she the misfortune only to see the worst?

Krista tapped at the door and Jill heard the command to enter. As she obeyed she was aware of the girl smiling and quietly moving away and found herself wishing she had stayed. She had no wish to face Bruno von Reimer alone, then she reprimanded herself for her cowardice. After all, what more could he possibly do to her?

Her mouth was dry as she stood with hands clasped before his desk, waiting for him to acknowledge her presence. But to her chagrin he made no pretence at looking up from the papers he was studying and once again she was aware that he had the ability to reduce her to the status of a student nurse anxiously awaiting approval on her first day.

She allowed her gaze to wander round the room and was surprised to find it attractive, in a masculine sort of way. There were shelves of text books she noted, some even bearing his own name. Yet another facet to his character which came as a surprise. The floor was carpeted, the blue matching the curtains and seeming to echo the dazzling blue-white of the scene beyond the window.

Studying his lowered head, she tried to imagine him in the surroundings of his home, in the elegance to which he was undoubtedly accustomed. Like an Austrian Lord of the Manor, she thought with wry humour, knowing his rights and demanding them in full.

With a start she realised that he was looking at her and she felt the colour stain her cheeks as if he guessed her thoughts.

'Ah yes, Nurse Sinclair. I trust you've had time to settle in. You were perfectly at liberty to take a little longer to recover from the journey.'

'Thank you.' Her chin rose. 'But I am quite ready to begin my duties. That, after all, is why I am here.' She threw the challenge and was annoyed to see it fall upon stony ground. He rose from his seat behind the desk and once again she was made aware of his muscular strength and her own vulnerability. He was the same and yet there was a subtle difference for here he was on his own ground and it seemed to give him an added strength.

She swallowed hard. 'There are one or two things I feel I should get clear. I had very little time to shop before we left England . . .' Why did her voice sound so far away? 'I realise now that I shall need to buy some clothes. If I could go into town some time, perhaps just for an hour.' She hesitated having no idea how long it would take to get there even.

'I see no problem, Nurse. You are free to use your off duty periods as you wish.'

Her mouth opened then closed again as she looked at him. 'I see. I hadn't realised . . .'

His brow rose mockingly. 'What, Nurse? That you would be free to come and go? Contrary to what you may believe you are not a prisoner here.'

'Not a prisoner!' Her anger burst forth. 'I fail to see how you can say that, under the circumstances.'

'I say it because it is the truth,' he said easily.

Her look rose sharply to meet his. 'And what about Martin? If I were to leave would you give me your word that he would still have the treatment you promised?'

He raised his eyebrows. 'It would be in his best interests, and yours, if you were to remain.'

'I see. In other words I was right.'

He shrugged. 'Interpret it as you will.' Then, to her annoyance he turned to his desk again. 'If there was nothing else, Nurse, I have a very full schedule ahead of me.'

'I . . . yes, as a matter of fact there is. It is the question of my uniform.'

He turned, scrutinising her appearance with such intensity, his gaze lingering over the slender curves of her body that she felt suddenly weak. 'I see nothing wrong with your uniform, Nurse,' he said sharply. 'On the contrary it is quite becoming.'

A soft gasp of exasperation left her lips as she

realised he was deliberately baiting her. 'That is hardly the point. If you will tell me where I can borrow or buy the correct uniform which is worn by other members of staff here . . .'

His gaze hardened. 'That won't be necessary, Nurse.'

'But surely.'

He cut her off, returning to his seat and picking up his papers. 'The uniform you have is perfectly adequate, I see no reason to change it.'

'I see.' She would not give him the satisfaction of arguing. 'In that case if you will acquaint me with my duties I can begin at once.'

He looked up impatiently, almost as if surprised to find that she was still there. 'I don't understand. There is to be no change. You will continue just as you did in England, giving your personal attention to Miss Klammer.'

'Of course, sir.'

'She seems to have recovered well from the more minor injuries and stood up to the journey surprisingly well. I'm particularly anxious to begin her new treatment.' He paced away and she could sense his uneasiness, even sympathise with it. So much was at stake.

'I am ready to begin at once. Will you wish to make another examination?'

'That won't be necessary. I've had most of the results of the tests and from those I'm virtually certain that the patient's inability to walk has a mental rather than a physical origin.'

Jill's gaze flew up to meet his. 'You mean . . . that there is no reason why she is unable to walk?'

He drew a hand across his forehead. 'Technically none.'

'But then why?' Jill stared at him aghast. 'She is so young, she has so much before her, every incentive.'

'I'm well aware of that, Nurse.' He spoke with such force that she bit her lip.

'Of course, I'm sorry.'

But his hand dismissed her words. 'I can only believe that for some reason she is afraid to walk. Perhaps she is afraid to try in case she fails.'

'I've known of such cases,' Jill murmured. There was a haunted look in his eyes which seemed to pierce her very soul and she had to look away rather than witness it.

'Whatever the cause, it makes our task no easier. In some ways it can even make it more difficult. Physical illness is something tangible but this . . .'

Sunlight streaming through the window played on his hair and Jill felt her throat tighten suddenly. It was ludicrous that she, of all people, should offer comfort yet she heard herself doing so.

'I may not know Miss Klammer very well but of one thing I am sure and that is that she is very much in love.' Her voice seemed to fade and she had to swallow hard before she could go on. 'Surely you can persuade her.'

He frowned but didn't look up. 'I think you overestimate me, Nurse.'

'No, sir, I think perhaps you underestimate your-self.' She didn't know what made her say it. She was only aware that his head jerked up and he stared at her. 'There has to be a way,' she said, quietly. 'We must find it.'

He nodded and she saw the weariness in his face. 'As you say. I hope that bringing her back to familiar surroundings will help. Apart from that I have devised a programme of exercises and this is where you come in. I want you to devote your time and energy specifically to this one patient, is that clear? She likes and trusts you, which is important.'

Jill heard the sound of her own hollow laughter ringing out. 'Trusts me?' She shook her head. 'Maybe now, but would she, if she knew the truth?'

His expression grew taut. 'There is no reason why she should ever learn it. My only concern is that she should be well again. Nothing else matters, nothing. Do you understand?'

She shuddered, afraid yet at the same time angry, as he held her powerless yet again. 'Oh yes, Herr Doktor, I understand perfectly. I understand that you will go to any lengths to get what you want.'

'As long as you appreciate that, Nurse, there is no more to be said.' He turned to his desk and she knew she was being dismissed. Blindly she stumbled towards the door, glad that he couldn't see the tears of frustration which welled up in her eyes.

CHAPTER SEVEN

JILL found herself slipping with surprising ease into the ordered routine of the clinic during the days which followed. The work load, though, not arduous by St Kit's standards, was sufficient to keep her occupied not only physically but mentally as they began the new treatments, and for that she was grateful.

She also found pleasure in a growing friendship with Krista, based in the beginning on an enjoyment of the girl's extrovert nature which seemed to give her an ability to cope with work which, though often rewarding, could also be depressing. That, and the fact that she seemed to be the one person who could reach Martin as Jill no longer could.

Having spent the morning trying to persuade Helga that the new exercises combined with a gentle course of massage would be to her advantage, Jill felt drained. The sessions were never easy but the sight of the once attractive legs becoming thinner and the girl's face more ashen were all the incentive Jill needed to fight her patient's growing irritability with what seemed to be a complete lack of progress.

Her eyes were bright with tears as she lay back exhausted against the pillows. 'It's no good. I'm never going to walk again, why don't we admit that now rather than go on with this . . . torture.'

Jill drew up the covers and struggled to keep her voice unemotional.

'Nonsense. We've only just begun. Surely you're not going to give up so soon without even a fight.'

'But I am so tired.' She brushed back the strands of hair. 'And it is all for nothing.'

'It's to be expected that you will feel tired at first. Gradually, though, you'll feel stronger. Each day the exercises will seem a little easier until you find that you can cope with them quite well. But the thing to remember is that at this stage you must let me do the hard work for you. We have to wake up those muscles and encourage them to do their own work.'

'You make it sound so easy.'

'No.' Jill bit back promises which she was only too well aware might prove unfounded. 'No, it won't be easy and it may take time, but you have so much to fight for. Surely it is worth trying, for the sake of the man you love?' She straightened up, every muscle in her own body aching with tension.

The blonde head moved restlessly against the pillows. 'Yes, I suppose you're right.' Jill felt a twinge of alarm at the lack of conviction this approach usually brought. 'Where is Bruno? I haven't seen him today. He will be coming to see me?'

'Yes, of course. But I happen to know there was a new admission, a child, so I dare say he has been held up for a while.' She rearranged the covers. 'Look, you get your rest now. That's an important part of the treatment too, you know. I'll come back later.'

She made her way along to Martin's ward, seeing his slim figure out on the balcony with the other patients who were watching the brightly-clad figures negotiating the distant slopes. Approaching, she found her own gaze also drawn to it. The view was beautiful and she found herself falling more and more in love with this country. The sun fell across the mountain now and lit the valley below. It was a dazzling world. But she drew herself up sharply. She mustn't get to love it too much, mustn't get to love anything about this place. Yet wasn't it already too late, she asked herself silently.

To Jill's relief she saw that Martin was talking to Krista. It was the girl who saw her first as she looked up, smiling a greeting. Martin turned slowly, the animation she had seen in his features only a moment ago dying. He said nothing as Krista rose to her feet.

'Oh please, don't go,' Jill said but with a rueful smile the girl looked at her watch. 'It's a temptation to stay, but I'm afraid I must. I do have other patients.' Her blue eyes sparkled down at Martin and Jill saw the swift flicker of disappointment in his face.

'You'll come back though?'

'But of course, as soon as I'm free. But now I leave you to talk to your sister. You are very lucky to have her here you know.'

His gaze watched her leave before he turned sullenly to Jill who took the chair beside him. 'Yes, I am, aren't I?'

She tried not to let herself be hurt by the coldness in his voice.

'How are you feeling?'

His gaze narrowed. 'Let's not go over that again. What does it matter how I feel? I'm stuck here aren't I?' With a swift movement he got to his feet and crossed to the balcony rail.

'Martin, what is it?' She followed, battling with feelings of helplessness and was shocked to feel him flinch at her touch. Slowly she withdrew her hand and he stared at her for what seemed like an eternity until suddenly he brushed a hand against his brow and shook his head.

Alarmed by his pallor she said quickly, 'Martin, for heaven's sake, tell me what it is.'

Just for a moment he seemed to be unaware of her presence and she could see a stricken look in his eyes. Then it cleared and he laughed sharply. 'It's nothing. Just for a minute I thought . . .' He seemed to be avoiding her gaze. 'I'm fine, but then, there's nothing like a change of scene to make you forget your troubles is there?'

She tried to ignore the thrust. 'Has there been any news yet about the results of the tests?'

'As a matter of fact von Reimer was here this morning.'

'And?' Her heart beat quickened. 'Martin, what did he say?'

He looked up at her. 'If you must know he says it's possible he can operate.'

'Oh, but that's marvellous. When?'

He frowned. 'I don't know. Soon I suppose. He didn't make any promises but then his sort never do. It's always safer not to commit yourself, isn't it?' His voice was sharp and she had to force herself to smile.

'That's defeatist talk. Look . . . is it too late . . . I mean will the offer of the scholarship still be open?'

'God knows. But in any case what's the point in even thinking about it until I know whether the operation is a success or not. If it isn't then the question doesn't arise does it?'

'I simply think you should consider the possibility.'

'Oh, for heaven's sake, Jill, just leave it.' His voice shook. 'Can't you see that just at this moment I don't even want to look that far ahead.'

'You never used to be a pessimist.'

'No, but then things have changed haven't they?' He turned abruptly away and she bit back the words which rose to her lips. She knew it was useless to try and talk to him. He had become completely un-reachable and every attempt only seemed to drive them further apart. She was at the door when he called her name.

'Jill!'

She turned quickly to see him standing, white-faced, a hand pressed to his head.

'Martin, what is it?' She started back to him. 'Are you in pain?'

For a long moment he didn't move but stood looking at her then, slowly, she saw him shake his head and with a feeling of dismay she saw the familiar sullenness return.

'No, it's nothing. Just leave me alone.'

Wordlessly she turned and left the room, closing the door behind her and as she leaned against it for a moment she realised that she was trembling.

It was her free afternoon and she had been contemplating going down to the village for the past few days. Now the thought became a driving force. She must get away, anywhere, if only for a few hours. Perhaps the fresh air and a change of scene would help to relieve some of the tension which was beginning to make her head ache.

She was just wondering whether she would be able to find the road down to the village when Krista waylaid her. The girl had changed out of her uniform and Jill had to admire the stunning effect of the smart navy trousers topped by a thick red sweater. It was typical of the clothing worn by both locals and tourists in the area and it was easy to see that it was practical as well as attractive.

'I hardly recognised you,' she confessed. 'Somehow the minute a nurse changes out of her uniform she seems to take on a totally different identity. I always found it at the hospital dances back home. There were times when I even passed my best friends. It makes me wonder if we aren't all cast in exactly the same mould.'

'I'm afraid it's true,' Krista laughed. 'But it makes me appreciate all the more the times when I can become the real me again if only for a little while and however much one loves one's work, it is good to get away.'

'Unfortunately I don't seem to have any of the right clothes with me.'

'Well, that's easily remedied.' Krista's shrewd eyes scanned Jill's slender figure. 'I'm just going to the village. Why not come too. There are plenty of shops. You can buy what you need and it will give me a chance to show you around.'

The invitation was too good to be missed. She hadn't been looking forward to venturing far afield on her own. 'Can you give me ten minutes just to slip into some outdoor clothes?'

'But of course. There's a bus in half an hour. I'll wait for you by the main doors.'

In less than that time Jill joined her, having changed quickly into trousers and her thickest sweater and an anorak. The bus journey was in itself an enchantment for her as she watched skiers twisting and turning between the snow-laden pines.

'They make it look so easy. I'm afraid I've never done more than the nursery slopes and even then I wasn't very good at it.'

'It needs much practice. Out here we begin skiing as very small children. Perhaps if you stay you can take lessons. The Herr Doktor, he is expert.'

'I'm sure he is,' Jill murmured, drily, then frowned. 'And Miss Klammer?'

'Oh yes, but she is . . . was, best known for her skating.'

Jill pretended she hadn't noticed the correction but somehow it stayed in her mind as the bus made its way along a road banded high with snow until they turned at last into the village square.

She shivered as an icy wind drove down from the mountains taking her breath away and was only too pleased to let Krista guide her towards the many attractive and varied shops. She was surprised by the number of tourists who had found their way to this small village but it was easy to see the attraction it had over some of the bigger ones. They spent a happy hour choosing tailored pants and a couple of thick sweaters, one in scarlet the other in a deep blue, as well as an anorak more suited to the climate. Admiring the effect in the mirror, Jill scarcely recognised herself. She crushed a matching woolly hat over her curls and pulled on a pair of mittens.

'I'll wear these now,' she decided, and the assistant happily parcelled up her other clothes.

It was amazing the difference the new outfit made to her jaded spirits. Or perhaps, as Krista had said, it was just good to get away for a while. Whatever the reason she felt happier, as if a weight had been lifted at least temporarily from her shoulders. It would be there waiting for her again when she returned to the clinic of course but for now she had a few hours in which to escape.

They sat first of all in one of the small cafés drinking coffee and eating slices of rich chocolate gateau and afterwards mingled with the tourists, many of whom were sadly shopping for souvenirs to take home. They went to see the local church with its impressive spire and then paid a visit to the heated open-air swimming pool.

Jill laughingly turned up the collar of her anorak as she watched the few enthusiasts splashing happily. 'I don't think I'll risk it until I'm more acclimatised,' she laughed. Then the thought came that she had no idea whether she would even be here that long.

Krista studied her watch, her expression falling. 'Oh dear, I have to be back on duty again this evening. It's time to catch the bus if I'm going to make it in time to change. Look, why don't you stay? There's so much to see and it seems a shame for you to come back for my sake.'

It was true, the very thought of returning made her spirits sink. 'Would you mind? I've no reason to get back and I'm not sure when I'll get the chance to come again.'

'Of course I don't mind. I'm happy for you to see something of my country. If you're sure you can find your way back.'

'I'll manage and the bus will drop me right at the clinic.'

'Well, then, I'll leave you to play at being a tourist.'

As Jill waved her off she thought, 'If only that were true.' Then she called out, 'Would you mind calling in to have a chat with Martin if you have time. He's a bit low and I don't seem to be able to cheer him up but I know he looks forward to seeing you.'

'I'll be glad to.' Krista sped away towards her bus but not before Jill had noticed the faint touch of colour which had risen to her cheeks. It gave her something to think about as she made her way slowly along the narrow streets and again, later, as she returned to the café to drink more of the delicious coffee and sample some of the apple strudel.

It was bliss to be alone. She was scarcely aware of the lengthening shadows as they began to cast a blue-grey light over the snow, or that the sun had gone leaving a trail of red-gold in the sky. It was only when she saw the small pin-pricks of light dotted about the slopes that she realised with a sense of alarm that it was almost dark. She had been so entranced that she had completely forgotten the time.

She began to walk briskly toward the bus stop, passing beautiful, deep-eaved houses which were so typically Tyrolean. She had to sidestep quickly to allow a horse-drawn sleigh to pass. The wind was bitingly cold now and she was glad of her new clothes as she drew up the hood of her anorak.

But at the bus stop she learned to her dismay that the last bus had already left and there would be no more until morning. 'Oh well, I'll just have to walk,' she exclaimed to the man who listened sympathetically to her stumbling German and raised his hands smiling.

She turned away, remembering vaguely that the road wound its way up from the village through the woods. The trouble was, in daylight it had seemed a charming prospect which now, in darkness seemed less so. But there was no alternative. She dug her mittened hands into her pockets and began to walk, her breath fanning white into the crisp air. Above her head, the sky was diamond-studded, like a shawl draped over the mountains. There was an awesome beauty about the country that she would never forget, she thought, and sighed. If only she could have been here under different circumstances.

She had been walking for about half an hour when she paused to take her bearings. It was further than she had thought and now the only sound was her boots crunching deeper into the snow and the wind blowing through the pines. The lights of the village lay far behind and eventually even they were lost. Breathless, she paused, trying to thrust back the first ripples of panic. Her feet and fingers were beginning to feel numb. Was it possible she had somehow managed to take the wrong path? She stood looking about her with an increasing sense of dismay. She could wander out here all night, or worse still, freeze to death. Oh, why hadn't she had the sense to return with Krista?

Resolutely she began to walk again. She seemed to have made little progress when the car's headlights cut through the darkness. It was still some distance away or, at least, so she had imagined until it came round a bend and, with a cry of alarm, she realised that she was directly in its path.

Instinct gave her speed. Without thinking, she leapt towards the side of the road only to discover to her dismay that the snow was banked too high. She felt herself slipping backwards. Her boots couldn't find a hold and she crashed to her knees hearing the car's engine come ever nearer. Desperately she flung up a hand to shield her eyes from the brilliance of the headlights unable to do anything except wait, frozen with horror as it bore down upon her. She closed her eyes and heard the driver jam on his brakes then waited for it to hit her. She felt sick and heard herself cry out in terror but, by some miracle, the crash didn't come. The wheels spun and stopped only inches away and she half lay, half sat in the snow as the car's door opened and she was vaguely aware of the tall, shadowy figure as it got out and strode quickly towards her.

Even before he could speak some premonition dawned upon her and she shivered as she looked up into Bruno von Reimer's taut expression. Angrily he bent towards her and she felt herself hauled unceremoniously to her feet.

'I might have known.' His voice rasped angrily. 'What in the devil are you playing at now, Miss Sinclair?'

She tried to move but couldn't. For some reason she was trembling violently and knew that it was not entirely from shock. His arms were about her, supporting her and she was conscious of the warmth of his body beneath the thin shirt. She tried jerkily to free herself but her knees felt ridiculously weak and, as if sensing it, his voice cut coldly in upon her.

'Do you go around asking to be killed. Have you any idea just how close you came to it?'

She stared up at him and to her chagrin felt the tears fill her eyes. Why, oh why, did it always have to be like this? He was like some demon haunting her steps. Angrily she tried to thrust him away.

'If you must know I missed the last bus and I was walking back to the clinic. I was scarcely to know that you were likely to come hurtling along the road like a maniac.' Shock mingling with anger made her speak more sharply than she had intended and there was a throbbing in her ankle where she had knocked it as she fell.

His dark gaze narrowed as he stared at her. 'I think you're being a little hysterical, Nurse, and I would remind you that this is a road. I had every right to be on it which is more than can be said for you.'

She gasped. 'And just where was I supposed to walk?'

'You might have tried the correct road.'

Her mouth opened and closed in vexation. 'I thought this was it.'

'That depends on whether you want a leisurely stroll. At a guess it would take you about two hours and it isn't to be recommended unless you know it well, Nurse, which you don't, and certainly not at this time of night.' He nodded in the direction from which she had come. 'You obviously took the wrong turning. The quickest route is about half a mile back and it would get you there in a quarter of the time.'

'Well, at least I shan't make the same mistake again,' she snapped ungraciously, only to feel his grip tighten on her arm.

'You're damned lucky there will be a next time.'

His gaze shifted as she winced and rubbed at her ankle. 'You're hurt. Let me take a look.'

'No.' She retreated hastily. 'I'm fine. It's just a bruise.'

'Even so, I can hardly leave you out here to hobble the rest of the way back to the clinic. You'd better get in.'

She tried to protest but his hand was on her arm and before she knew what was happening she was in the passenger seat and he went round and eased his frame in behind the wheel. Suddenly she was even more conscious of his nearness. The confines of the small sports car seemed to emphasise it even though she sat on the furthest edge of her seat. Then she chided herself for her foolishness. The only danger was from her own emotions which seemed to be stirred to foolish proportions as she studied his profile in the semi-darkness, seeing the arrogant set of his jaw. She trembled, turning away quickly to stare out of the window then a wave of doubt hit her.

'But this isn't the way to the clinic.'

He turned briefly to look at her, his hands relaxed on the wheel. 'No, it isn't.'

Her fingers clenched tightly in her lap. 'Then where are we going?'

His attention was fixed on the road ahead but she saw him frown. 'I happen to have an important appointment which I have no intention of breaking, so I'm afraid there's no alternative but for you to come along. Don't worry, Nurse, I'll get you back safely.'

She sat rigidly in the seat, battling with a feeling of resentment as he seemed to be taking charge yet again. 'If you had only told me, I could have walked quite easily.'

His gaze flickered briefly in her direction. 'Frankly, Nurse, you are a menace I'd rather keep off the roads.'

She shrank back into the shadows, hating him for that self-assurance when he managed somehow to rob her so easily of her own. 'I suppose it doesn't bother you in the least that people will be bound to gossip, however inaccurately?'

His expression was hidden from her yet she thought, incredibly, that she heard him laugh. 'You're right. It doesn't bother me in the least. I've long since learned not to fight the inevitable. Perhaps you should do the same.'

All the responses which rose to her lips seemed to die in a strangled sob of exasperation as she turned away. Once, she sensed that he glanced in her direction but she refused to give him the satisfaction of returning the look, sitting stiffly, as far away from him as she could.

He drove in silence and she became aware, with an increasing feeling of alarm, of the miles being lapped up.

'You might at least tell me where we are going,' she insisted, after a lengthy silence. 'And surely if you have an appointment I shall only be in the way?'

'I suppose you have a right to know where I'm

taking you. As a matter of fact I'm going home, to visit my mother.' He turned to look at her and she had the uncanny feeling that he was laughing at her. 'I do have a mother you know.'

'No, I didn't, and you surprise me,' she retorted.

His mouth twitched. 'Well, in that case, I insist you meet her, just to put your mind at rest.' He changed gear, his hand brushing against her knee and sending a shock wave through her. 'We'll be there soon. It's just outside Innsbruck. It's quite a drive but I try to make it as often as I can.'

She was aware of the nervousness flooding through her. 'But you can't take me to meet your mother. I mean . . . what will she think? It's not as if I'm even dressed for the occasion.'

His gaze flicked over her. 'What should she think? My mother is always pleased to have visitors, she sees few enough people these days. As for your appearance, you look fine to me.'

She fell silent. He was giving her no choice in the matter but what did it matter whether she was dressed for the occasion or not. The visit had been forced upon her and that's all it was after all, a visit. He wasn't asking her to become part of his social background. It was Helga, the woman he loved who would do that, who had been born to it. Her throat tightened and she pressed a hand to it, starting as he spoke.

'You're very quiet, are you sure you're alright?'

She was glad of the darkness which hid the sudden flush in her cheeks.

'Yes, I'm fine, just tired. It's been a long day.'

'Strange, I didn't take you for a liar, Nurse Sinclair,' he said softly, watching as her head jerked upwards.

'I'm not a liar.'

His brow rose. 'You were deep in thought and those thoughts were troubling you.'

She swallowed hard. If he knew how much they troubled her and that he was the cause! 'If you must know, I was thinking about my brother.'

'Ah, yes of course. I see.'

In the darkness she uncrossed her fingers and was glad he didn't pursue the matter. They drove in silence again for some minutes until he said suddenly, 'We're here.'

The car's headlights illuminated the long sweep of drive and as they drew to a halt Jill's eyes widened as she stared with dismay at the sight before her. Before she could move he was holding open the passenger door and, with his hand beneath her arm, she stepped out, gazing up at the rugged magnificence of the stonework before her. She hung back.

'It's a castle!'

He followed her gaze. 'I suppose it is, but it's not very grand you know. Oh it may have been once but now it's upkeep is crippling. We fight a constant battle against damp and draughts and icicles hang in the baronial hall rather than tapestries.' He spoke lightly yet she sensed there was no real humour in the words. 'I'm afraid it's a losing battle.'

'Then why do you do it?'

He smiled. 'I have my reasons. Perhaps you will understand them better when you have met my mother.'

She allowed herself to be led through the vast doorway and found herself standing in a large, echoing hall. Her anorak was taken by a man-servant who appeared silently, as if from nowhere, and she stared up at the stonework of the walls where portraits, undoubtedly from their likeness past generations of the family hung.

'Is my mother at home, Franz?'

The old man smiled, pointing to the staircase. 'The Baroness is in her rooms, Herr Doktor. She will be pleased to see you again so soon.'

'Then we will go up to her.'

But Jill hung back. 'I've no wish to intrude.'

'I assure you, it would be no intrusion. On the contrary, if my mother knew I had brought a guest and hadn't introduced you she would be most offended.'

'But I am hardly a guest. You may recall that I had no wish to come.'

'Even so, now that you are here, would it not be a little ungracious to deny a lonely old lady the pleasure of seeing a new face? She suffers poor health and seldom goes out.'

Faced with such arguments Jill realised she could hardly refuse and even before she was really aware of it they had mounted the stairs and he was pushing open one of the doors.

It opened on to an apartment and she stepped

inside with the uncomfortable feeling that she had no right to be here. After the bleakness of the hall the sudden brilliance took her breath away for it was a room full of warmth and colour. A huge fire burned in the great hearth, the flames reflected in mirrors and a huge chandelier. There were flowers and paintings. But it was to the tiny figure who had risen to utter a cry of pleasure as they entered that her gaze was drawn and as she watched she saw the fragile figure being embraced with a tenderness of which she had never imagined Bruno von Reimer capable.

They spoke briefly in their own language until he glanced in her direction and suddenly Jill found herself the object of a careful scrutiny by the vivid blue eyes. She felt suddenly self-conscious as the tiny figure, so slender, so elegantly gowned, moved towards her. The Baroness was a beautiful woman whose age was and would always remain, indeterminate, despite the silver-grey hair. Jill's mouth felt dry then the woman smiled, her hand outstretched and to Jill's surprise she found herself being embraced warmly.

'Wilkommen. Welcome, my dear. You must forgive me, my son tells me you are English and I am a little out of practice.'

'No, please, it is I who should apologise, for intruding.' Her glance went above the Baroness's shoulder to Bruno who watched enigmatically. She wondered what he had said to his mother, she wanted to explain but she was given no opportunity as she found herself being put swiftly at ease by this gentle lady who was so unlike her son in every respect that it seemed almost inconceivable that she could ever have borne him.

'But it is no intrusion, Miss Sinclair. I am always pleased to see Bruno's friends.'

Jill was conscious of the mocking glance before she turned deliberately away.

'He works so hard,' the Baroness was saying. 'Ach, but you also, you have come to nurse at the clinic?'

So he had told her that much. 'Yes.' She was led towards the fire and unthinkingly accepted a glass of wine which Bruno proferred. Their fingers touched and she experienced a momentary sensation as if an electric current had run through her before she drew her hand away quickly.

'You will stay for dinner.' The Baroness smiled and Jill glanced up sharply. Now he would have the perfect opportunity to make some excuse, to say that they must return.

'But of course, mama.'

She bit her lip. He accepted, she noted, without even deigning to consult her then, as she saw the look of pleasure which lit the older woman's face, she knew that she was being ungracious.

'Good. I am so pleased.'

'But I'm afraid I'm hardly dressed for it . . .' Jill began, only to have her protests dismissed as the blue eyes passed approvingly over her appearance.

'She look very pretty, does she not, Bruno?'

'Indeed she does.'

Jill felt the colour surge in her cheeks as she became aware of his close scrutiny then he set down his glass and straightened up.

'If you will forgive me for a moment, there are some papers I must take with me to the clinic when I return.'

The Baroness watched her son go and Jill saw the look of pride in the attractive face, yet it was overshadowed. A thin hand indicated the satin covered couch. 'Come and sit beside me, my dear. I so seldom have visitors since my husband died and my own health became less good. I'm afraid it makes me a little selfish.'

Jill sat and gave her attention more fully to the beautiful room. Despite its elegance it was obviously lived in, had a homeliness which seemed to reach out and envelop her in its warmth. Then she shook herself mentally. What was the point in becoming attached to something when she would have no part in its future? And yet it would be so easy. She frowned. 'I think I should tell you that I am here under false pretences, at least . . .' she stumbled helplessly. 'Herr von Reimer didn't invite me here as a guest, he simply offered me a lift . . .'

'Ach.' The Baroness smiled, her slender hand gesturing understanding. 'My son, but he is always so. Sometimes I think he is like a whirlwind. One has no choice but to do as he wishes. It is easier.'

'You are very fond of him.'

'He is a good son to me. He works hard, too hard. But, like his father, Bruno also has a dream. The clinic, the idea was his father's you know. But it was left to Bruno to make it a reality and though I perhaps should not say it, his father was a fine man with much skill, Bruno has something more, a kind of genius. But you know this of course.'

'Yes.' Memories of those occasions when she had seen him tending his patients flooded in so that she answered without hesitation. There was a tenderness, a kind of magic in him which could dispel the fears in even the most timid, the most sick. It was a side of his character which kept catching her unawares. She looked round her desperately. 'You have a beautiful home. You must be very proud of it.'

'Indeed.' It has been in our family for four hundred years. It would break my heart to leave it, but alas,' a frown disfigured the gentle features, 'it becomes more and more difficult to keep.' Her glance rose to the portraits. 'Of course, we lost much during the war. My husband . . .' her voice trailed away. 'Bruno was very young but sometimes I think even he remembers. They were hard times, Miss Sinclair, but perhaps because of them we cling even more closely. Our roots, our history is here. It may seem strange to you, I know it is hard for the young to understand such things, but I feel it is important that all this should go on, will go on, in my son.'

Jill felt her hand tremble as she brushed a strand of hair from her eyes. 'I understand very well. Such things are important.'

'Yes,' the blue eyes looked into hers. 'Somehow I thought you would.'

Jill's gaze fell. But what if it couldn't go on. What if Helga never walked again. What if there could be no sons, no continuity?

She looked up with a start as the door opened and rose to her feet as Bruno came towards them. She was unaware of the pallor in her face until he looked at her sharply. 'Are you unwell? Perhaps the fall . . .'

She seized at the excuse. 'Yes, as a matter of fact my ankle does ache a bit.'

The light from the fire played across his face and she saw his expression change. 'I'm sorry. Perhaps I shouldn't have brought you here after all. It was a mistake.'

So he had realised that for himself. The thought rang, hollowly, in her brain. He could see now that she was awkward, ill at ease. Suddenly she felt very tired and realised that in fact her leg did ache. But not as much as the ache in her heart. He shouldn't have brought her here, given her this glimpse of that side of his life in which she could never have any part.

'I'll take you back.'

He spoke to his mother. Whatever he said the Baroness seemed to accept their sudden departure without surprise though she made no attempt to hide her regret. As they were leaving Bruno hurried on ahead to the car and as Jill waited the older woman caught her hands and kissed her cheek.

'I'm sorry you must go, my dear. Come again, I should like that very much.'

Jill returned the kiss with an affection which was

in no way feigned. Even in so brief an acquaintance there was something about this woman whose fragile looks far belied an inner courage, which drew her. But as she hurried out to the car Jill knew that it was impossible. She would never come here again. The next woman to do that would be Bruno's wife.

Depression settled over her as they rode back to the clinic in virtual silence. Once or twice she was aware of him turning to glance in her direction but he said nothing and she huddled in her seat. She wasn't even aware of the passing miles. Part of her wanted them to go on for ever and another part wanted only to get out, to escape from his nearness.

The car slid to a halt and, with a start, she realised they had arrived. She fumbled for the door catch but even as she did so his arm moved across her, preventing her getting out.

'Wait.'

Bewildered she sat back fighting the feelings of misery. Her throat ached from the effort of holding back the tears. 'I'm very tired.'

He turned to her in the semi-darkness. She could make out his profile in the dimmed light of the clinic but his features were indistinct.

'I know you're tired. I've been thoughtless, I shouldn't have taken you to my home, but we've got to talk, Jill. I think it's time, don't you?'

He had used her name. A tear found its way on to her cheek. She was glad he couldn't see it. 'Let me go. It's very late.' She hadn't any strength left with which to fight him any longer. His nearness, the very sound of his breathing was doing things to her, her brain ached with confusion but she mustn't fall into the trap, she mustn't.

She heard his sharp intake of breath then felt his hand on her arm and before she knew what was happening he had drawn her close and his lips were on hers. He kissed her with a gentleness which left her senses reeling, brought her numbed senses surging back to life. With a sob she flung caution to the winds, raising her face willingly to his, her lips parting hungrily. The strength of her emotions shocked her as desire coursed through her. He moved, drawing her closer. She was helpless to fight, didn't want to fight. Then, the full horror of what she was doing jerked her back to reality. No, this was crazy. What was she doing? She wrenched herself away, her hands against his chest. How could he forget so easily that he was committed to another woman? Because he had no conscience must he credit her with none either? Or was this all just part of the game? She thrust him away.

'No, don't touch me. Let me go.'

He froze as if she had struck him then his hand jerked away and she fell back. For a long moment he was silent then, in a voice she scarcely recognised, he said coldly, 'You're right, for a minute I almost forgot . . .'

She didn't wait to hear anymore. With a sob she fumbled at the door, thrust it open and almost fell out in her haste to escape. She ran up the steps, knowing he sat there staring after her. She ran blindly through the swing doors until she reached the safety of her room where at last she gave way to the tears. Her head throbbed, she felt bruised, physically and mentally, and she had only herself to blame. How could she be such a fool? But then logic played no part in love. She had wanted his kiss, always had and always would, as long as Bruno von Reimer was around.

CHAPTER EIGHT

JILL saw very little of Bruno during the next few days but even though she told herself that that was exactly the way she wanted it, it didn't explain the feeling of misery which seemed to envelop her like a thick, grey cloud.

Digging her hands into her pockets she climbed the slope, her boots embedding themselves in the thick layer of snow. It was hard going but she was glad of the exercise, anything which helped to drive her thoughts away, yet somehow, even out here they seemed to follow. Not even the act of flinging herself determinedly into her work had managed to dispel the memory of what had happened and even now it filled her with angry confusion, anger at her own stupidity in not having foreseen it, for having allowed herself to believe, even for a moment, that anything had changed. It hadn't and never could and she wasn't a child any longer, she was old enough to know that wishing didn't make things come true.

She lifted her face to breathe in the cold air. She had to get away or go crazy. And now there was an added complication. She hadn't counted on taking an instant liking to the Baroness. How could such a gentle, fragile woman ever have borne such a son, she wondered, and knew that she would feel a real sense of regret at not seeing her again.

She stared into the distance but wasn't even aware of the rugged beauty before her. Somehow she had to get away. There was Martin of course, but once he had had the operation . . . Please God let it be a success, she prayed silently. After that there is nothing to keep me here, nothing and no one, least of all Bruno von Reimer she thought. But as she turned to begin retracing her steps she shivered. Though she might escape physically, some part of her would always be held here, a prisoner. She would never be totally free.

In fact, she wasn't due back on duty for another two hours yet but already she found herself dreading returning and it wasn't entirely her reluctance to see Bruno again which was the cause. There was a growing concern for Helga Klammer who seemed to be making little or no progress in spite of the therapy. Jill had been nursing long enough to know that patience was of the essence in this profession. God knows, she had often preached that particular sermon to Martin. But for some reason she felt uneasy where the girl was concerned. They had made a good beginning, that was what made it all the more confusing. It was as if suddenly it had all come to a halt, as if she had given up hope. But why? Was the failure in some way her own, Jill wondered, yet surely not? She had done everything possible, she *wanted* the girl to get well.

She made her way slowly back to the small, private ward and was about to push the door open when she heard the sound of voices and laughter. For a moment she froze then, slowly, she entered and her brows rose. Far from looking pale and depressed, her patient was at this moment not only laughing but her eyes had a sparkle and the cause of it was not particularly difficult to find. Jill's gaze flew from the gorgeous bouquet of red roses to the blond-haired young man who was standing beside the bed. He was tall, over six feet and powerfully built yet for all the strength which seemed to emanate from him, Jill couldn't help but be aware of the gentleness with which he took the other frail hand in his.

Jill stood motionless at the door. They were totally oblivious to her presence as they looked into one another's eyes. She felt like an intruder and, for some inexplicable reason, she felt suddenly uneasy.

She turned to leave and in that moment Helga looked up. Jill saw the colour flood into the girl's cheeks and wondered at it as she heard her say, 'But you are not due back on duty for another hour, Nurse.'

'No, that's right.' Jill moved towards the bed,

pausing to sniff the heady perfume of the roses. The young man shuffled in embarrassment but Helga made no attempt to release his hand, to which she clung with an almost child-like intensity. 'As a matter of fact I went for a walk but it started to snow so I came back rather earlier than I had intended.' She smiled. 'I thought you were supposed to be having a rest but as you're not perhaps we can begin the new exercises.'

She saw the hesitant look which the girl flung in the young man's direction and the way his hand tightened over hers. 'I ... I'm not ready ... Tomorrow perhaps.'

'No, no Helga.' To Jill's surprise the young man bent over the girl, his voice softly persuading. 'What use to put off until tomorrow what I know you can do today. For my sake.'

The generous lips trembled and Jill sensed the tears which hovered as the girl looked uncertainly up at him. 'For you, then I will try.'

Jill drew in a breath. 'Good. It will tire you a little so that you must rest a little longer afterwards.'

'I do not mind being tired if only I could be sure I shall be well.'

'But she will be well, will she not, Fräulein? I have told her so.'

'The doctors have every reason to believe it.' Jill heard herself say. 'This is what the therapy is for and there has already been a slight improvement.' She didn't add that she had hoped for more.

'There, you see.' A smile lit the handsome,

bearded features but there was no answering certainty in the girl's eyes.

'They all say it, but it is so slow. Sometimes I think they only tell me I shall walk again so that I don't give up hope.' Suddenly she covered her face with her hands. 'Oh Hans, you wouldn't lie to me. I couldn't bear it, to be a cripple for the rest of my life.'

'You will not be, liebling, I swear it. Please, don't cry.' He dabbed at her eyes with his handkerchief. 'There, that's better.'

With a sudden feeling of self-consciousness, Jill had to turn away from the look of tenderness in his eyes. She busied herself with an unnecessary re-arranging of the flowers and found herself watching the door and wondering what Bruno von Reimer's reaction would be if he were to enter the room now.

'I'm afraid it's time to begin Miss Klammer's treatment now. You'll have to leave but perhaps you can return later.'

'You will come?'

Jill felt a stab of pity for the eagerness with which the question was asked.

'Yes, I'll come, as soon as I can, if you promise to try and get well.'

'I will, I will, now.'

He nodded and bent to kiss her cheek before reluctantly releasing her hand. After he had gone Jill found it difficult to concentrate her patient's attention on the treatment and she found herself vaguely troubled by the effect the young man had

had though she tried not to show it.

She turned back the covers and carefully began the familiar pattern of exercises, of moving and gently coaxing the thin wasted leg muscles back into life. Her hands moved expertly, raising and lowering, massaging, her trained eyes always watching the girl's pale face for any signs of undue stress, until the prescribed time was up.

'There. I think that's enough for today. We don't want to overdo it.'

To her surprise Helga frowned. 'But I'm not in the least bit tired. Why can't we go on?'

'No,' Jill said gently. 'It's a good sign that you managed to cope with it so well but there can be too much progress too soon you know.' She smiled. 'Perhaps tomorrow we can go on a stage further.' She smoothed the pillows, checked the pulse and made the usual routine checks. 'You did very well.'

'Did I, really?'

'I'm very pleased with you. If you go on as you have today I'm sure we'll have you walking again in no time. The Herr Doktor will be delighted and you want that, don't you?'

Helga put down the brush with which she was brushing her hair and stared at her reflection in the small mirror. 'Yes of course.' Her gaze flickered towards Jill. 'Do you really believe I shall walk again by spring?'

Jill was aware of the sudden tightening of her throat. 'Anything is possible if you wish it hard enough.'

The mirror was lowered and a smile touched the pretty features. 'Oh, I do. I want to walk to my wedding.'

With shaking hands Jill gathered up her tray and moved towards the door. Somehow she managed to smile. 'Try to get some rest now. I'll be back later.' She closed the door behind her, leaning briefly against it and letting all the sensations of weariness and confusion wash over her. Spring wasn't so far away. The snow would soon be gone and the hills would be lush and green and dotted with alpine flowers when Helga married the man she loved.

She released her breath on a sob. Somehow, anyhow, she must be back in England when that happened.

She changed quickly out of her uniform into casual clothes, ate a light lunch even though it tasted like chaff in her mouth, and made her way to see Martin.

He was sitting out on the balcony and she saw, with relief as she went towards him, that he was looking, physically at least, much more like his old self again. He had even acquired a tan.

As she watched, he was chatting happily to some of the other patients and she was pleased to see that he had discarded his dressing gown in favour of slacks, shirt and sweater as many of the other patients who were encouraged to walk in the grounds during the day did. In fact, looking at him now it was hard to believe any of that nightmare had actually happened.

'Hullo, Martin.'

The pleasure faded from his eyes as he turned and her spirits sank. Perhaps she should have stopped coming, she thought as she walked towards him, feeling the sun warm on her face. Then he surprised her.

'So you've come at last,' he said sharply. 'I've been waiting to see you. But of course I should have realised, there are more important things aren't there?'

The other patients drifted away leaving them alone and Jill was glad. She was tired and had never seen him in quite such a mood before. It was becoming more and more difficult to humour him, especially when, as now, his words were so unjust. She sighed and managed to smile.

'If you mean I have my work, yes I do, but I came as soon as I could get away.'

He flung away the cigarette he had been smoking and, for a second, had the grace to look shame-faced. Jill leaned against the rail. There was no joy to be had in scoring points. What had happened to their past relationship? They had always been so close, it just didn't seem possible they could have come to this.

She felt the wind stir her hair. Freed of its cap, the short curls flicked about her face and she brushed a hand through them as if it could ease the niggling headache. 'Was there something particular you wanted to see me about?'

'Does there have to be something particular?'

'No, of course not.' She turned to look at him, her eyes narrowed against the sun. 'You know I'm always glad to see you.' She nodded approvingly. 'You're looking better.'

'Am I?' he responded bitterly. 'Well, God knows why. It's not as if I'm getting anywhere. Just what am I here for?'

She frowned. 'What do you mean? You know why you're here, for treatment.'

'Oh really.' His sarcasm didn't escape her. 'It's funny, that's what I thought too. Perhaps you can tell me when it starts?'

Jill stared at him. 'But I thought Mr von Reimer had agreed to go ahead with an operation.'

'So did I but as you can see, nothing's happened.' His mouth tightened. 'Look, Jill, what's going on? How long are they going to keep me cooped up here?'

'I . . . I don't understand, Martin.' She shook her head trying to push away the vague feeling of uneasiness that was creeping up on her. He snorted impatiently.

'Well then, join the club because neither do I. But I tell you this, I'm sick and tired of waiting. If there's no hope then for pity's sake why don't they tell me instead of raising my hopes with promises which come to nothing. I could have got those back in England.'

'But I'm sure there is hope,' she protested. 'After all why would he have said so if it weren't true?'

His brow rose. 'You tell me. Perhaps he just

doesn't like admitting he was wrong. Well, I'm not hanging around much longer.'

Alarmed, she rested a hand on his arm as he half turned away. 'Martin, what are you planning to do? Promise me you won't do anything rash. Please, try to be patient. There could be any number of explanations for the delay.'

He whipped round to face her, thrusting her away. 'Oh, for God's sake spare me the lectures. I've heard them all before.' He moved away, leaving her standing at the rail. She called out after him.

'Martin, where are you going? What are you going to do?'

'If you must know I'm going down to the village. I feel like getting good and drunk and don't try to stop me.' He hurried away and as she stared helplessly after him Krista came to stand beside her, her gaze following him sadly.

'What am I going to do?' Jill turned to her.

'Let him go. After all it can do no harm. It might even help. The one thing I'm sure of is that you can't prevent him.'

In a daze Jill allowed herself to be led along to Krista's room where she accepted a cup of coffee, not because she wanted it but because it gave her something to do. 'I've never seen him like this before.' She stared down at the cup.

'He is afraid. That is natural.'

'It's more than that. He wants this operation so desperately but if it goes wrong ... Krista, I'm worried.'

The girl nodded. 'If it is any consolation, so am I. But he must fight this thing out for himself and if necessary he must come to terms with the fact that he may never be able to play the piano again. No one can do that for him, Jill, not even you.'

'Especially me it seems.'

'Be patient.'

Jill laughed mirthlessly. 'That's something I've become very good at preaching to others of late.'

'Then practise it. Whatever it is that troubles him, let him fight it in his own way.'

Jill looked at her. 'You care for him too, don't you?'

'Yes,' Krista smiled shyly. 'Yes I do, very much.'

'I'm glad. He needs someone.'

She shrugged. 'At the moment his greatest need is to find himself. Perhaps when he has done that . . . who knows? We can only wait and see.'

CHAPTER NINE

FROM the window of her room Jill watched the encroaching darkness without too great a feeling of alarm, after all, Krista was right, she told herself. Martin was a grown man and quite able to take care of himself.

But was he? The thought kept hammering at her brain and she bit her lip. In his present state of mind, was he capable of making any rational decision? It wasn't just the injury to his hand, there was the amnesia, that total blacking out of everything connected with the accident. It seemed to be eating away at him and, ironically, that was the one thing about which she couldn't tell him the truth.

'I shouldn't have let him go.' She murmured the words aloud as she saw that it was beginning to snow again, quite heavily. Already the mountains were lost behind the swirling curtain of white. She glanced uneasily at her watch then tried to settle to writing a letter home in an attempt to take her mind off Martin. It wasn't easy, trying to find the right words which would put their minds at ease when her own was in such turmoil. An hour later she abandoned the effort and after only a moment's hesitation hurried along to the ward to check whether Martin had returned. He hadn't, and she came to a decision.

Hurriedly she collected her anorak, mittens and a torch. She scribbled a note for Krista, pushing it under the door so that it would be found when she came off duty. Having done so, Jill left the clinic and began to make her way towards the village.

She hadn't counted on it being easy but the reality was far worse than anything she had imagined. The wind was icy and flakes of snow drove at her face, stinging and taking her breath away. Her boots slipped on the ice and as she stumbled the torch fell from her frozen fingers. Angry at herself for such clumsiness she knelt, searching in the darkness until her fingers made contact with the cold metal. She pressed the switch again and again then a sob of exasperation broke from her lips. Nothing. It was useless.

'Oh no.' She stared into the darkness trying to control the shivers which racked her body with such violence that her teeth chattered. Powder-fine snow dislodged by the wind showered down on her from the trees as she stumbled to her feet. For a moment she thought of turning back then some new thought came to her, filling her with terror. What if Martin was lying out there somewhere? She had to go on.

Shivering she plunged on feeling her boots sink into the loosely packed layer of snow. She tried to laugh at her own panic. If she kept to the road, sooner or later she must either find Martin, probably on his way back, or reach the village. He was probably sitting in front of a roaring fire and thoroughly enjoying himself. Then she remembered his mood when he had walked out and she tried to quicken her steps.

It wasn't easy. In the swirling whiteness everything looked different. She paused, breathing hard, feeling the cold burn into her lungs as she looked about her and only then did she realise with a gasp of dismay that somehow she had stumbled on aimlessly and had lost the path. Several hours of snow must have obliterated it and she had wandered on, head bent, without noticing.

The sound of her own breathing came back to her

through the eery silence. The great, feathery boughs of the pines hung over her head like a canopy through which moonlight filtered palely, emphasising the shadows before it vanished again. But it had given her time to realise that she had climbed upwards. Somehow she must make her way down again. Carefully she began to edge her way with awkward sidesteps down the slope. If only her hands and feet weren't so cold. She dragged off her mitten, blowing on her hand. Her boot crunched in the snow then, without warning, it happened. Her foot struck a hidden rock, grating against the ice-covered surface and she was plunging downwards. She heard a scream without even realising that it came from her own lips. Her hands clawed blindly for a hold but there was nothing. She was falling too quickly.

Her arm jarred sickeningly against something, sending a wave of pain shuddering through her but it did nothing to check the speed of her fall. She gasped, choking as the powdery snow flew around her then her foot caught against something. The impetus sent her rolling over and over. Lights flashed inside her head. She was aware of pain then nothing more as a merciful blackness claimed her.

She tried to move but sank back with a cry, resting her head against a tree until the wave of dizziness passed. Her anorak and mittens were wet, filmed with snow. She felt sick and her head ached but a cursory examination told her that luckily there were no broken bones. She had no way of knowing how long she had been unconscious, probably only seconds. Had it been any longer she realised with horror that she might not have woken up at all. It was freezing hard now and she knew that somehow she had to keep moving.

She tried to will her body to move but the effort was too much. She felt too tired, her head was spinning. Perhaps if she just rested for a moment . . .

Her eyelids jerked open as she realised that she was falling asleep. That was the one thing she mustn't do. People died in the snow. 'Must keep moving,' she muttered, the words scarcely coherent because she was shaking so violently with cold. 'Must find Martin.' She wasn't even aware that she called his name. Drawing up her knees she sat huddled against the tree, fighting back the waves of blackness which were crashing around her until finally she submitted and closed her eyes, just for a moment . . .

The lights hurt her eyes and she closed them tightly again as they intruded upon her peaceful oblivion. She heard voices too as she cradled her throbbing head against her arm. She cried out but the lights came relentlessly on, flicking through the trees above her head. Then suddenly they were all round her, dazzling, so that she lifted a hand to shield her eyes and heard someone call her name.

With a supreme effort she managed to find the strength to answer and then, as if from a long way off, she heard a familiar voice cry, 'Down here. She's here.' Then someone was hurtling down the slope towards her. Strong arms grasped her, hands passed gently over her. 'Thank God.' She was being lifted and knew then that she must be delirious because the face which stared so anxiously down into hers was Bruno's. His features were gaunt, his mouth tight set, but she was scarcely aware of anything except the sudden, blissful warmth which flooded through her.

There were other voices too, but only one which penetrated her numbed senses as she lay cradled against him. 'Don't move. You're safe now. I've got you.'

She tried to break free as her brain remembered. 'I must find Martin. I have to get to him.'

But the arms merely tightened around her. 'Don't worry. I'll take care of that young man. Just you sleep.'

She closed her eyes and sighed. Everything was all right. She was safe now.

CHAPTER TEN

THE next twenty-four hours passed without her being fully aware of them. There were moments, of course, when she knew that someone came and stood beside the bed, held her hand and brushed the hair from her face but it was all vague, too unreal and all she wanted was to sleep again.

By the following morning she knew she was much better. 'I feel such a fraud lying here,' she confided in Krista who had popped in to see her. 'I'm perfectly capable of going back on duty. In fact I'd rather. I hate being idle.' It left too much time for thought and her thoughts made uncomfortable bedmates. So much of what had happened was still a blur yet other things were so real, things which she told herself were impossible.

'Make the most of it,' Krista urged, smiling. 'You gave us all a fright. In any case the Herr Doktor has ordered that you remain in bed, at least for today.'

'Oh, did he indeed.' Jill knew that her cheeks flooded with colour.

'He was so very worried. We all were. It was late when I found your note and realised what had happened, and when you still hadn't returned several hours later it was Herr von Reimer himself who called out a search party and insisted on joining it himself.' Her gaze flickered over Jill. 'I've never before seen him look as he did when he knew what had happened.'

Jill shuddered, the full horror momentarily returning. 'I fell.' She frowned, brushing a hand through her hair. 'Somehow I must have wandered away from the road. The torch was broken and I couldn't see.'

'Indeed you were very lucky. A little longer and it would have been too late. The Herr Doktor said so himself and it was he who found you.'

'Oh no,' she groaned. 'He . . . he actually found me?'

'And brought you back to the clinic. He stayed with you for several hours until he knew there was no danger and finally he was persuaded to go to bed. I tell you, I never saw a man look more troubled.'

'Angry, more like,' Jill muttered and Krista grimaced.

'You may be right. At any rate he spent a long time with Martin who was certainly not happy afterwards. But he deserved it, I think.'

Jill clasped a hand to her mouth. 'Martin. Oh what a fool I am. I'd completely forgotten. Is he alright?'

'Perfectly. This is what I am telling you. Apparently he returned to the clinic not long after you left. He was drunk, more than a little. It's a miracle how he managed to find his way here but by the time the Herr Doktor had finished with him he was very much sober again.'

'Oh no, poor Martin.'

'Poor Martin indeed. He is not at all a happy young man and now he has the headache too, but it is as much as he deserves.' She looked at her watch. 'I must go. I'm on duty again in a few minutes. I only came to see how you were.'

'I'm fine, apart from a few bruises. It's Martin I'm worried about, Krista. None of this would have happened if he hadn't been so keyed up about the operation. He's got it into his head that it has been delayed purposely and I must say,' she frowned, 'it seems so unfair.' She saw the frown which flickered across Krista's face. 'What is it? You know something. Something is wrong.'

Krista bit her lip. 'I only know that the operation *was* scheduled some time ago and then, for no apparent reason, the Herr Doktor postponed it at the last minute.'

Jill stared at her, suddenly aware that her heart was beating uncomfortably fast. 'But why? I don't understand. What possible reason could he have?'

'That I don't know. It was Herr von Reimer's decision. Only he could change it.'

Jill felt as if an icy hand had suddenly touched the nape of her neck. 'I don't believe it. How could anyone be so cruel . . . so vindictive. He knows how much this operation means to Martin.'

'I'm sure he has his reasons.'

'Oh yes, I'm sure he has,' Jill whispered. 'And I mean to find out exactly what they are.'

Krista turned anxiously to look at Jill from the doorway. 'Perhaps I should not have said anything but I thought you knew.'

'No.' Jill struggled to swallow the lump in her throat. 'I only knew what Martin told me, that the necessary examinations had been made and he had been told that an operation was possible.' Her face was white as she considered the implications. What had changed? *Had* anything changed. She had to find the answer and there was only one place she would be able to do that.

Dressing was a much slower process than she had

bargained on. She discovered bruises she hadn't known existed until now and her face, when she looked in the mirror, looked white against the starkness of her uniform. Even the slightest movement made her head throb again and she clung for a moment to the rail at the foot of the bed until a wave of dizziness passed then she made her way slowly to the office and tapped at the door.

He was speaking on the telephone and standing with his back to the door as she answered his call to enter. He was wearing a neat, grey suit and she was conscious of his height, the muscular strength of him as she waited impatiently, an uncomfortable feeling in the pit of her stomach. Was it really possible that she had actually lain in his arms, that he had held her so tenderly? She reprimanded herself sharply for the thought. It had all been part of the delirium, there was no other explanation.

He turned and she saw his jaw tighten.

'What the devil are you doing out of bed. I thought I left orders that you were to remain there for at least twenty-four hours.'

The room seemed to be revolving. It took every ounce of concentration to stand still, to meet his gaze. 'Yes, you did. But I am perfectly well and I must talk to you.'

'Surely it could have waited?'

'No, Herr Doktor, it can't wait.' Her gaze faltered. 'I suppose I should thank you for saving my life . . .'

His hand rose and she saw his expression darken. 'You were a damn fool, and so was that brother of yours. Do you realise you might have been killed?'

'I didn't stop to think.'

'No, I can well believe that, Nurse.'

She flinched. So much for his concern. It wasn't much in evidence now. Her chin rose. 'Even so, thank you for what you did.'

'Forget it. And now, if that's all, I'm very busy.' He was dismissing her, he had turned away but anger made her stand her ground.

'I'm sorry but that isn't all. It's about Martin I must speak to you.'

She swallowed hard. 'Is it true that you had decided to perform the operation and then cancelled it?' She didn't know what she had expected, a denial, anger, anything but the stony glance he turned upon her.

'It is perfectly true.'

She gasped. 'But why? How could you? To raise such hopes.' Tears of anger pricked at her eyes. 'You . . . you're inhuman.'

'You may be right.' A nerve pulsed in his jaw then, before she could guess his intent he had drawn out a chair and was pressing her down into it. 'Sit down before you fall down and listen to what I have to say.'

She tried to protest. 'I doubt if there is anything you can say which will change my opinion of you.' If her head hadn't been reeling so much she would have walked out. As it was she had no choice and he was quick to take advantage of the fact. He stood over her, his mouth a taut line.

'You've made up your mind about me, haven't you.'

'On the contrary, Herr Doktor, you made it up for me and nothing you have ever done has given me any reason to change it.'

'Well, perhaps it's time you knew the truth. I didn't raise any hopes. If anyone did that it was your brother.'

She jerked her gaze up to his. 'But you said you could operate.'

'I said it was possible.'

'Oh . . . you're quibbling. What's the difference?'

'Quite a lot,' he said softly.

'But that still doesn't explain why you put it off, why you purposely delayed.'

He studied her for a long moment through narrowed, dark eyes. 'You want the truth?'

'Of course,' she snapped. 'Why else do you think I'm here.'

'Very well.' He drew a breath. 'I *can* operate, that much is true, but until now I have delayed because although there is a good chance I can restore full mobility to Martin's hand, there is also a risk, a slight one maybe but a risk nonetheless, that something could go wrong.'

She absorbed the words in silence for a moment. 'And if it does? Surely that's not the end of it.'

'I'm afraid it is. If I operate and fail he will never play again.' He saw her whiten and moved quickly. Vaguely she was aware that he was beside her, holding a glass of water. 'Here, drink this.'

She obeyed, mechanically, then pushed the glass away. Somehow his nearness made it impossible for her to think clearly. 'Why didn't you tell me?'

He shrugged. 'The decision wasn't yours to make.'

'But ... surely Martin must know the risk involved?'

'He does know, now. I told him last night, after we had sobered him up.'

She rose unsteadily to her feet. 'I must go to him.'

But his hand came down on her arm. 'No. This is one decision he must make for himself. Haven't you done enough?'

Wearily she brushed a hand through her hair. 'I don't understand.'

'No, I don't suppose you do.' He looked at her for a long moment before turning abruptly to his desk again. 'I have told him I want his decision by morning. If he agrees, the operation will be performed immediately.'

'And ... how soon will we know?'

'Not long. A few days.'

Not long. It seemed an eternity. Her hand was on the door handle when he spoke again with a sharpness which stung. 'I would prefer it if you didn't see your brother. It is important that he remain quiet.'

'But he is my brother.'

'He is also my patient, Nurse. Must I remind you where your first duty lies?'

She bit back a protest, seeing the hard set of his mouth. 'No, Herr Doktor, you needn't remind me.'

Then she turned on her heel and almost ran from the room before he could see the tears in her eyes.

She woke next morning with a headache. It was her day off but instead of taking advantage of it to enjoy the luxury of a lie-in she got up, wallowed in a warm, scented bath and dressed slowly. She still felt exhausted and it showed in the dark circles under her eyes. On this of all days she would have preferred to be busy.

She made her way along to the dining room where she refused breakfast and took just strong, black coffee instead. She carried it across to the table where Krista sat. Her friend looked at her anxiously and eyed the cup disapprovingly.

'You should try to eat something.'

'I know, but I can't.' She ladled sugar into her coffee, stirring it mechanically. 'I've lain awake most of the night wondering how Martin must be feeling.'

Krista pushed her own plate aside. 'If it is any consolation I saw him this morning.'

Jill's spoon clattered noisily into the saucer. 'How is he? Oh, if only I could see him.'

'He is fine,' Krista said gently. 'He asked for you.'

Jill's eyes widened. 'Did he? Well, that's something new.'

'I explained to him that visitors were not allowed. He understood and seemed not to mind.'

No, that was more like Martin, Jill mused with a sense of irritation. She would be the last person he wanted to see, blaming her as he did. Then she thrust the thoughts away. Her reasons for wanting to be with him were purely selfish, she needed to put her own mind at rest. 'I feel so useless.'

'I too,' Krista murmured and, for the first time, Jill noticed the drawn look in her friend's face and felt a pang of pity.

'Yes, I'm sorry, I forgot. You care too, don't you? I've been so wrapped up in my own problems ... Forgive me.'

'There is nothing to forgive. It is I who am being foolish, after all it isn't even as if Martin knows I'm around.'

'On the contrary, I think he's very much aware of you and I'm glad he has you. He needs someone and obviously it isn't me.' She sighed. 'Perhaps when it's all over ...'

'But when it is over perhaps he will no longer even need me.' Krista stared bleakly into her coffee then forced a smile. 'But all that matters is that he should be well again. If he is able to play then we must be grateful, nothing else is important.'

'Yes.' But Jill shivered as if something or someone had walked over her grave. Nothing else was important. 'Do you know when the operation is to be?'

'This afternoon.'

'So soon?'

'Dr von Reimer doesn't wish to delay any longer. Apparently Martin sent word of his decision to him late last night and they spent an hour talking together afterwards.'

Jill hid her surprise, not that anything Bruno von

Reimer did should surprise her any more. 'I hardly dare think what Martin must be going through.'

'As a matter of fact, now that the decision is finally made he seems quite calm.'

'But what if it goes wrong?' Jill murmured.

'He knows the risks. He has made his choice. But in any case it will be a success. We must both believe it.'

Jill pushed her cup away. 'Well, I can't just sit and brood. It will be hours before we know anything.'

'What are you going to do?'

'I think I'll go on duty. I've got to make myself useful and I don't care how as long as I don't have time to think.' She looked at her watch. 'I suppose we should know something by this evening.'

'I expect so. I can always let you know.'

'Thanks.' Jill smiled. 'But I mean to see Martin for myself once this is over and this time no one will stop me, not even Bruno von Reimer.'

CHAPTER ELEVEN

IN spite of her resolve, she had to make a conscious effort not to keep looking at her watch but it wasn't easy, and it was almost as if her own mood transmitted itself in some way to Helga.

The girl was sitting in her wheelchair at the window when Jill arrived. She flung a glance over her shoulder and her mouth compressed sullenly.

'Oh, it's you. I don't feel like doing any exercises today.' The blue gaze lingered defiantly and Jill paused in the act of turning back the covers.

'Aren't you feeling well?'

'Perfectly. I just don't feel like it that's all, and what difference will it make if we leave them until tomorrow?'

'Well, quite a lot as a matter of fact.' Jill managed to say, as she moved the table aside. 'We don't want those muscles to tighten up again or forget what we've already taught them. It would be a shame after all the work you've put in. They've become lazy.'

Helga sighed. 'And I should like to be lazy too.'

'I know how you feel, but don't you think we should persevere, having come this far. You know you're beginning to make progress and the doctors are very pleased.'

'They think there is no reason why I cannot walk,' came the snapped response, and the blue eyes filled with tears. 'You too think it, I can see it in your face.'

Jill felt a flicker of alarm but managed to suppress it. 'The important thing is, do *you* think it, Helga? Have you made up your mind not to try, perhaps because you are afraid you won't succeed.'

The generous mouth trembled. 'I want to walk.'

'Yes, of course you do, and that's why the exercises are so important. I know it isn't easy . . .'

'No, it isn't.' The response came, sharply. 'But what do you or anyone know of it. It isn't you who sits here each day, having someone else move your useless limbs for you. Why don't you just tell me the truth, why don't you just say I shall never walk again.'

'Because it isn't true. You *have* made progress, surely you must sense that for yourself.'

'Sometimes I do, but then it seems so slow. I begin to think it is only my imagination.'

'But it isn't,' Jill insisted. 'Surely you believe Dr von Reimer?'

'I know he wouldn't lie to me,' Helga said in a small voice.

'Then there you are. How can you even think of giving up now, when you have so much to fight for? Would you like me to ask him to come and see you as soon as he is free?'

'No.' The swiftness of the rejection both puzzled and alarmed Jill but she managed to hide it as she began gently to brush the long, blonde hair. 'As you wish. There, is that better?'

Helga stared unsmiling at her reflection in the mirror. 'I look like a ghost. How could any man find me attractive any longer?'

Jill swallowed the restriction in her throat. 'The man who loves you finds you attractive, and you are. You're feeling depressed now but it will pass. For his sake as much as your own you must try.' And for my sake too, she thought as she stood at the window. Her glance rose to the clock on the wall. Martin would be in theatre now. She seemed to be praying for so much these days.

She stared out at the lake. The ice was thick and someone was skating on it. Some of the patients were sitting in chairs watching and suddenly an idea sprang into her mind. She drew in a breath and turned to Helga.

'Look, how would you like to go out, just for a while?' She saw the widening of the blue eyes, the hope and the doubt which flickered in them. 'It's such a beautiful day, I don't see that you could come to any harm.'

'Go out? But . . . is it possible?'

For one terrible moment Jill asked herself that same question. What if she was making a hideous mistake, yet some inner instinct drove her on. 'Why not? We can dress you in some nice warm clothes, wrap a thick blanket round you and tuck a couple of hot water bottles in beside you then I could wheel you out into the grounds. Not for long of course,' she added warningly, 'but who knows, perhaps we could gradually increase the time you spend out there. What do you say?' She was surprised to see the blue eyes fill with tears.

'Oh, I should like that very much. It is what I have wanted above . . . above almost everything. I feel so trapped, but how can you possibly understand that?'

'I do understand, very well as a matter of fact.' Jill murmured, hiding her face rather than let the girl see the expression in her eyes. 'Look, how about wearing this lovely red sweater?' It was a slow process but eventually Helga was dressed and wrapped in a warm blanket. As she tucked it in the girl's hand closed over Jill's.

'You have been so good to me. I feel that you are my friend and not just my nurse. I know I haven't been a very good patient.'

'Nonsense.' The irony of those words struck her yet again. 'I'm only doing my job.'

'No, it is more than that. I can feel it.'

Jill turned away, biting her lip, 'I want you to walk again and I know you can do it. You must, for . . . for Dr von Reimer's sake. He cares very much.' She broke off, tormented by the memory of his kiss, and involuntarily her fingers rose to quench the sudden burning. But nothing could remove the guilt of knowing that she had actually welcomed it. Not even the knowledge that it had meant nothing to him.

Her hands were shaking as she tucked the blanket round Helga's knees and wheeled her along the corridor and out through the glass doors into the fresh air.

It was cold, their breath fanned white before them but the sun was shining as she manoeuvred the chair along paths recently cleared of snow. In a few weeks from now there would be spring flowers. Time was running out.

She turned her steps towards the lake and came to a halt. This was a favourite place with the patients and she joined them now, watching the few skaters who were cutting patterns across the ice.

It was the sound of a sob which brought her out

of her reverie and, to her horror, she saw that the girl's knuckles were clenched white against the chair. With sickening dread, Jill realised what she had done and her eyes filled with remorse.

'Oh no. Forgive me,' she begged. 'This is the last place I should have brought you to. I just wasn't thinking.' She made to turn the chair. 'I'll take you back.'

Helga's face was ashen as she stared across the lake but she shook her head. 'No, wait.' Her hand trembled as she pressed it to her mouth.

'I didn't think.' Jill's voice trailed away miserably. 'I forgot that you used to skate. Believe me, I wouldn't have done this for the world.'

'But there is nothing to forgive.' The thin hands were still taut, her face pale but she looked up at Jill. 'I know you didn't do it purposely, and yes, it is true I once used to skate.' Her mouth quivered into the semblance of a smile. 'Very well as a matter of fact. But I see now that I was wrong.'

'What do you mean . . . wrong?'

The thin hands rose. 'I see now that I have been trying to push that part of my life away from me, as if it were over. And maybe it is, for me, but I can't go on closing my eyes to things I would rather forget.' She frowned. 'I should like to stay here for a while, alone.'

Jill hesitated, then nodded. The damage was already done and to refuse now might only make things worse. Her heart thudded painfully at the thought of having to face Bruno von Reimer with the folly of her actions. He would never cease to make her pay for what had happened on the night of the accident and now this . . .

'I'll leave you just for a few minutes then we must get back. We don't want you getting over-tired.'

But Helga didn't even see her walk away. Her gaze was fixed on the skaters, a haunted expression in her eyes.

Digging her hands into her pockets Jill took the path which ran round the lake. Walking with her head bent she almost collided with the tall figure who came towards her.

'Nurse Sinclair.'

She looked up into the troubled face of the young man who had visited Helga some days earlier. 'Herr Veiber.' A trace of a smile flickered across her lips.

'I went to the ward but Helga is not there. I looked everywhere.'

The note of anxiety in his voice shook her. 'No, she isn't there. I took her for a walk. You'll find her down there,' her hand gestured towards the lake and she saw the look of incredulity which spread across his handsome features.

'Helga is down there, watching the skaters?'

Jill nodded miserably. 'The blame is entirely mine. I acted completely without authority.' She brushed a hand through her hair. 'I'm afraid I just didn't think until it was too late and when Miss Klammer expressed a wish to remain, well . . . I felt it might do more harm than good to refuse.'

His strikingly blue eyes looked down into hers and

he asked, 'Who is to say you acted unwisely?'

She frowned, her gaze going to the solitary figure in the distance. 'I understand that Miss Klammer was a skater of some ability before ... before the accident.'

He smiled. 'That is so. As a matter of fact we skated together many times and in the last Austrian Championships we took the silver medal. It was not the gold of course but we told ourselves that next year ...' He broke off seeing the stricken look in Jill's eyes. 'Who is to say it may still not come true? It is still possible that she may walk again?'

'There is no medical reason why not.'

He nodded slowly. 'Sometimes fear is the worst enemy, the only enemy. But there comes a time when reality must be faced even though we may not like what we see.'

She grimaced. 'Somehow I doubt that Dr von Reimer will see it that way. I acted foolishly. The patient may come to considerable harm because of it.'

'You must not torment yourself so.' He frowned. 'May I go to her, talk with her for a while?'

'Why yes. But only for a few minutes. We must get back and obviously I shall have to report my actions.' She shivered and was glad he hurried away leaving her to return to her walk.

They were sitting together when she returned, but even from such a distance she could see the flush which coloured Helga's cheeks and then felt a pang of alarm as it seemed they exchanged angry words. She began to hurry towards them but even as she did so she froze, held by a sudden terrible premonition. As she watched she saw Hans rise to his feet and, with the utmost gentleness he bent and took the girl in his arms. Some sound broke from Jill's lips and was stifled as she pressed a hand to her mouth. She could only watch helplessly as he drew Helga from her chair and held her in his arms, tilting her face up to his as he kissed her slowly and lingeringly and, as Jill watched, the kiss was returned in a way which left her in no doubt at all that they were in love.

Her senses reeled. She knew she should move but couldn't. Her feet seemed to be rooted to the spot. It was like a dream, there was a quality of unreality about it. It wasn't possible. Helga was going to be married to another man, yet how could she deny the eivdence of her own eyes?

She saw Hans move, slowly, putting Helga from him. Her brain registered the action and she wanted to call out, to stop him but it was too late. She saw Helga thrust aside the blanket and sway.

Jill began to move but it all seemed to be happening in slow motion. Then she saw Hans Veiber gesture roughly to her to be still. He alone seemed to be aware of her. Helga was staring up into his face, her own ashen, her mouth moving soundlessly and then, incredibly, as he held out his arms, Jill saw her move. A single step and she swayed, crying out but he made no move to go to her. Then another step and she fell into his waiting arms crying softly then laughing.

Somehow, Jill forced herself to move and she heard the young man speak as he cradled Helga in his arms. It was as if a shock wave hit Jill and she could only stare in disbelief.

'I love you. I love you.' He brushed back the blonde hair and kissed away the tears. 'We'll be married soon, as soon as you are strong.'

Helga laughed. 'I am strong now. I don't want to wait.'

'But only until the spring and we have a lifetime before us.'

They kissed again and Jill moved forward like an automaton. She couldn't believe any of this was happening. Helga couldn't talk of marrying this young man, she was engaged to Bruno. She was aware of the girl watching her, her face alight with joy.

'You were right,' she said softly. 'You said I would walk if I wished it hard enough.' Her hand reached up to clasp the stronger one and there was a look of adoration in her eyes.

Somehow Jill managed to find her voice as she looked helplessly from one to the other. 'I don't understand.'

Hans laughed. 'But it is simple, we shall be married as we had always planned and, who knows, we may even skate together again.'

Jill struggled to speak. 'But you are in love with Dr von Reimer.'

The blue eyes widened. 'Ah yes, I have always

loved Bruno, but not, I think, as you mean. He is very dear to me. I have known him since I was a child. That is why he took me to England to see my parents when Hans was skating in America.' Her face darkened. 'And then there was the accident. But it is over now. I shall walk again, I know it.'

Scarcely aware of what she was doing, Jill left them alone together and made her way back to the clinic. She wasn't even conscious of the tears streaming down her face, wasn't aware of anything except the dull pain in her heart.

Bruno wasn't to marry Helga. Her brain said it over and over again. But then why, why had he kissed her as he had, only to reject her. Why had he let her believe? The answer rang like a knell in her heart. He had warned her but like a fool she had refused to believe that even he could be so cruel. He had sworn to pay her back. Her heart felt as if it had turned to ice. He had used her. Oh yes, perhaps he even found her sexually attractive but how he must have laughed as he sensed the power he had to arouse her willingness to be kissed. She pressed a hand to her burning cheeks. How easy she had made it for him and how he must have laughed at her protests.

Choking on a sob she went to the bathroom and sluiced her face in cold water. It took her breath away but seemed to act like a stimulant, clearing her senses. She stared at her reflection in the mirror and was appalled by the stricken image which stared back at her.

'I've been a fool,' she told herself. 'But not any more. I've learned my lesson.' Her mouth compressed then, as a tap came at the door, she frowned. She ignored it but it persisted until she crossed angrily and flung it open. Words of reproach died on her lips as Krista stared at her anxiously.

'Are you alright?'

'What? Oh yes, just tired that's all.'

'Well, I brought news to cheer you. Martin has had the operation and is safely tucked up in bed. You can see him if you like, though only for a few minutes.'

Jill received the news, feeling it thread its way through her numbed senses. 'How is he?'

Krista smiled. 'Still sleepy, but that is to be expected. Apart from that everything went well.' Her own relief was obvious. It showed in the sparkle of her eyes and Jill found herself thinking, 'Martin will be a fool if he lets her go.'

'I must go to him.' She should have put on a little make-up, a touch of lipstick to hide the ravages of the shock but Martin wouldn't notice, she thought as she hurried to his room.

He was lying with his eyes closed when she entered, quietly, and approached the bed. He looked pale and his hand was covered by a dressing but apart from that he was resting quite normally. Her trained mind registered such things as she stared down at him and it was some moments before she realised that his eyes were open and he was watching her.

'Hullo,' she smiled. 'Welcome back.'

He was still drowsy and licked his lips. She moved automatically to offer him a few sips of water then as he lay back he brushed a hand against his brow.

'It's nice to be back, I think.'

She laughed. 'Give it time. I expect you're still feeling a bit groggy but that's the anaesthetic. By morning you'll be fine.'

He was looking at her strangely. 'That's not exactly what I meant.'

Jill felt suddenly uneasy. It was almost as if he was seeing her properly for the first time but she dismissed the thought. That was probably the after-effects too. Patients were often a little confused after an operation.

'I gather everything went very well,' she said.

'Yes, so Krista told me. She popped in for a few seconds. She's a nice girl.'

'Well, I'm glad you noticed,' she quipped, but his face was serious and she bit her lip. 'Look, we don't know the results yet, of course, but there's every reason to suppose . . .'

'It's alright, Jill.' He cut her off but for once there was none of the sharpness she had come to expect. 'I went into this knowing the score. Your chap von Reimer made jolly sure of that.'

'He isn't my chap,' she said abruptly and he frowned.

'Sorry, I must be even more confused than I imagined.'

'Obviously.' Her hands were shaking and she had

to clench them together. 'I can't think what gave you such an idea.'

'Nor can I. But then, I seem to have been confused about a lot of things just lately, don't I?'

She evaded his glance, aware of a sudden tightening in the pit of her stomach. 'Do you?'

'Look at me, Jill,' he said, so sharply that her gaze flew to meet his. She tried to move away but his hand caught at her arm.

'You should be getting some rest you know.' She tried to make it sound like a professional opinion but he ignored her saying brusquely,

'For pity's sake, don't make this any harder for me than it already is.'

'Don't.' Her voice shook. 'Please Martin, don't say anything. There's no need.'

'Isn't there?'

She saw the look in his eyes and shook her head.

'For God's sake, Jill, how could you have let me go on all these weeks . . . these months? I've even lost track of the time. Letting me believe . . .' He broke off and she covered his hand with her own.

Suddenly her own eyes brimmed with tears. 'It won't serve any purpose, Martin.'

'Won't it? Well, I think you're wrong. I couldn't live with my conscience if I didn't clear it up between us. How on earth have you borne it? You must have been through hell all this time, hearing me accuse you of something for which I was responsible. Why, why didn't you tell me the truth?'

She shrugged. 'You had enough to bear.'

'But what about you? That other girl who was involved. That was my fault and you've taken the blame.'

'How did you find out? When?'

He pressed a hand to his eyes. 'I don't know exactly. The awful thing is that I suspected.' He closed his eyes briefly, opening them again to stare at her. 'The accident was a total blank but afterwards, gradually, I began to remember. Oh, not all of it, just brief moments, glimpses, but it was all so unreal. I saw myself at the wheel but I couldn't believe it. I was so sure it had been you. It was your car . . . Not that that's an excuse. God knows I had no right.' His face was pale but he wouldn't listen to her as she tried to stop him. 'And then it began to get clearer. Oh, I didn't want to admit it, not to myself, not to you. So I just pushed it away. Can you ever forgive me?'

'There's nothing to forgive,' she said quietly. 'And if you must know, the girl, Helga Klammer, is going to walk again. She's even going to be married in the spring.'

She saw his mouth quiver into a smile. 'Well, that's marvellous. It's that chap von Reimer I suppose?'

'No.' Jill released her hand. 'Actually she's marrying someone quite famous. Someone she has known for a long time. Hans Veiber.'

His eyes widened. 'You don't mean the skating champion?'

'The very same. They even hope to be skating

together again before too long and I think there's every chance they'll do it. So you see, you've nothing to worry about. Everything has worked out just fine.'

His narrowed gaze scanned her face. 'Has it, Jill? Has it for you?'

'But of course.' She managed to laugh. 'After all, I've had these glorious weeks in Austria. I've seen you safely through your op and I believe . . . I really do believe that everything will be alright. So,' she took a deep breath, 'I've decided it's time I went back to England again and did some real work. St Kits can use me I'm sure.'

He frowned and, for a moment, she thought he meant to argue. 'If you're sure.'

'Yes, I am. It's what I want. You know I can't bear to be idle and in any case I can give Mum and Dad a full report. You know how they worry.'

'I suppose you're right. When do you leave?'

'As soon as I can get a flight. Tomorrow probably.'

'So soon? But will von Reimer let you go?'

She was at the door, knowing that if she didn't get out soon her smile would fade and she would give way to the tears which threatened to burst like a flood. 'Why not? I'm no further use here. In any case I'm a free agent, aren't I?' She smiled. 'You'll be in good hands and if you've any sense at all, brother, you'll not let a good thing like Krista get away. She adores you, though heaven knows why.'

He was laughing as she closed the door behind

her and the sound rang in her ears as she leaned against it and gave way at last to the tears which would be held back no longer.

CHAPTER TWELVE

SHE was awake just before dawn, cold and exhausted, having slept only fitfully. She still had no definite plan. Nothing was clear any more, she thought bitterly, except that she had to get away before anyone could try to stop her or even begin to suspect her intentions.

Dressing quickly, she finished the packing she had begun last night. Clothes were strewn over the bed. She threw them into the case carelessly. Soon it would be light, the night staff would be going off duty and everyone would be astir.

If there had been some means of getting to the airport last night she would have taken it but as it was impossible she had had to wait. The hours had been full of mental agony but at least she had discovered that a car would be going into Innsbruck this morning, as it always did so that the driver could collect supplies or bring new patients back to the clinic, and she would beg a lift and be away before anyone could even notice her absence.

She snapped the locks on the suitcase, checked

her passport and her purse. Mercifully, she had enough for her ticket. There would be very little left over but if necessary she could always ring her parents, or even Keith at the hospital for more money. She pushed the thoughts away. They were of the least importance at this moment.

Picking up the case, she made for the door. She didn't want to disturb Krista but as she tiptoed along the corridor she paused to slip the note she had scribbled last night under the door. It was brief but there had been little to say and it was better this way, better if there were no arguments or attempts at persuasion. She knew Martin would be in good hands and that was all that mattered.

Quietly, Jill let herself out through the glass swing-doors, gasping as the cold morning air hit her. She was glad she had decided to wear her anorak and the tailored slacks. Once back in England she would probably put them away and revert to all the old familiar things. But, with a pang, she knew that things could never be the same again.

A pale orange glow was beginning to light the sky as she walked down the steps and made her way along the drive, her feet crunching over the fresh layer of snow. Looking back, she could see the lights in the wards and knew a faint sense of regret. Some things she would miss she thought wryly, but the rest was something she had to try to forget. At the moment she couldn't believe it would ever fade but there was her work and that would help. Perhaps even Keith . . . If he still wanted her. At least if she married him there would be no storms, no heart-ache.

She turned as the hospital car pulled up at the gates. The driver grinned and flung open the door for her and she climbed in.

'You leave early, fräulein.' He glanced up at the sky. 'It will be a fine day.'

He was right. She stared through the windscreen seeing the shadows already stealing over the mountains as the sun began its track across the valley. The trees stood like diamond clad sentinels, their branches gleaming with snow. It was hard to leave so much beauty behind.

'Yes, it will be a fine day,' she said and accepted a cigarette. Her fingers were unsteady as she lit it and his own, but it gave her something to concentrate on and the warmth soothed her a little. Why was she shaking? She was free wasn't she? In a few hours she would be back in England and she would never see Bruno again.

The landscape was a blur as she stared through a mist of tears. Perhaps in time she would be able to look back and feel nothing but right now it was all too close. She had been foolish enough to fall for a man whose only interest in her was to get his revenge. Well, he had certainly had it.

The driver was shaking her gently and she came back to reality with a start.

'We are here, fräulein. This is as far as I can take you. I have to collect medical supplies and take them back to the clinic. But the airport is only five minutes walk.'

In a daze she thanked him, climbed out, dragging her suitcase after her. She stood watching as he drove away and looked about her. The streets were fresh and clean. The snow had been cleared into mounds, and a tantalising smell of coffee reminded her that she hadn't eaten.

A glance at her watch showed that there was at least two hours before her plane left so she made her way into one of the little cafés and ordered a cup of coffee. Sitting at the window she sipped the hot strong liquid. The day nurses would be going on duty just about now. Perhaps Krista had found the note but by the time it became general knowledge she would be airborne and away. As for Bruno von Reimer, no doubt he would merely wish her good riddance. She didn't deceive herself into thinking that even when ... if, he discovered the truth, he would feel any regret.

She drew a deep breath as she rose from the table and walked out into the street again to make her way slowly to the airport. When she got there it was quiet, only a few early travellers were dotted about the attractive, airy lounge. She bought a selection of magazines from one of the book stalls, scarcely even glancing at their titles, then made her way to one of the chairs.

It seemed an eternity before the tannoy system burst into life announcing that passengers for the flight to London should now proceed to the appropriate gate for boarding. She gathered up her suitcase and began to make her way forward, ticket and passport in hand.

There were a few late arrivals. The doors swung open and she was vaguely aware of a figure bursting into the lounge as she crossed to the desk then, just as she held up her tickets, a hand fell on her arm, gripping it like a band of steel with such force that she gasped with pain and stared up into Bruno's grim features. The colour drained from her face. Suddenly her knees felt weak. It wasn't possible, it was unfair. A few more minutes and she would have been away beyond his reach. Violently she tried to thrust him off but his grip merely tightened and she felt a shudder pass through her as, without a word, he drew her mercilessly away.

'Just where do you think you're going?' he demanded. 'What do you mean by skulking off like that?'

She stared at him. Even now the sight of him was enough to stir her emotions and she was conscious of his strength as he led her inexorably towards the doors.

She drew herself up, angrily. 'If you must know I'm catching the next flight to England and there's nothing you can do to stop me. You've had all the fun you're going to get out of me, Mr von Reimer.'

A cynical smile hovered about his lips, his mouth was hard. 'Are you sure there's nothing I can do about it? We'll see about that.'

And before she could guess what he intended he had grasped her suitcase and was propelling her forcibly out of the lounge. Protests died in a maze of shock. Tears of anger blinded her so that she stumbled but his grasp merely held her, forcing her on.

They were outside. Vaguely she saw the dark limousine drawn up, recognised the driver and even as her brain whirled she thought it strange since he usually drove himself. Then, for the first time she noticed that her captor wasn't his usual immaculate self. He wore no tie or jacket but had pulled a jumper over his shirt. There was even a hint of stubble on his chin. For one fleeting moment she thought of telling him the truth and of confounding his actions but her voice wouldn't come. Even if it had, she doubted it would have made any difference. He may not have loved Helga as a future wife but he still loved her and as far as he was concerned someone, anyone would have to pay for what had happened.

He jerked the door of the car open and she began to struggle wildly. Without a word he threw her suitcase inside, lifted her bodily and flung her in after it before getting in beside her. He uttered some sharp command to the driver and the car moved away. She knew it would be useless to call for help. The glass screen had slid to a close between themselves and the driver and she felt the hand still firmly on her wrist.

She lay back breathing hard. 'Where are you taking me? This isn't the road to the clinic.'

'That's right, it isn't.' His mouth clamped into a rigid line and she closed her eyes, too tired to fight.

'Haven't you had your revenge yet?'

He didn't look at her. 'Not quite.' He spoke amazingly calmly she thought but sensed the threat nonetheless. Her heart was pounding but there was no way in which she could escape.

Later, she had no idea how much later, the car slid to a halt. He climbed out, jerking her after him. With a sudden tremor of fear she looked about her. They were high up in the mountains and she could see nothing but a small cabin. Her eyes widened and, to her dismay, she saw him speak to the driver and before she could open her mouth to protest the car moved away.

'What are you doing?' she panicked. 'Call him back.'

His narrowed gaze studied her calmly. He even smiled. 'I have no intention of calling him back and I might as well warn you that there's no one else around for miles so it won't do you any good to scream. Like it or not, Jill, we're stuck with each other.'

He had used her name. She frowned then he held her arm again and, like an automaton, she allowed herself to be led, stumbling, through the snow towards the cabin. He opened the door and they entered. She stared bleakly about her and she knew that, under normal circumstances, and in different company the surroundings might be pleasant enough, even more, they were luxurious. There were colourful rugs scattered about the floor and a fire was laid in the great stone hearth. She shivered and he let her go.

'It's cold but we'll soon get a fire going.' He bent to flick a lighter to the logs and within seconds flames leapt and the wood began to crackle filling the cabin with the heady scent of pine.

She was trembling and it wasn't entirely from the cold. Just what did he intend? Why had he brought her here? The questions must have been written in her face because as he turned his expression softened. He was looking at her in a way which made her legs feel like jelly.

'Take your coat off, Jill.'

Her hand went to her throat. 'No, I'm not staying here. I don't know what you have in mind but I have a plane to catch. You may have caused me to miss one but there will be another.'

He moved towards her and she retreated quickly, trembling. 'I don't think so!' His voice was soft. 'I said before that we should talk, you and I. This time I mean it. Like it or not, you don't get out of here until we've done so.'

Wildly, she looked about her but he had effectively sealed off her only means of escape by putting himself between her and the door.

'But this is . . . this is abduction.' Her voice was dry.

'So it is.' He smiled, then just as quickly his voice hardened. 'But don't make the mistake of thinking I'm one of those romantic heroes who will be swayed by a few tears into letting you go.' He saw her lips tremble. 'What's the matter, Jill. Afraid? That's good, because you have reason to be.'

She was afraid of her own emotions. Her body felt as if it was on fire as his eyes seemed to strip her. She gasped. 'Why are you doing this? What can you possibly hope to achieve?'

'Why are you running away?'

A sob caught in her throat. 'As if you need to ask.'

'But I am asking, and I mean to have an answer.'

He was close, so close that she could feel his breath on her cheek. She jumped as his hand came down on her shoulder, caressing her neck, and she closed her eyes feeling suddenly faint.

'Let me go.'

'But I can't do that.'

Her eyes flew open again as she stared at him. 'You have no choice, you can't keep me here a prisoner.'

His brow rose. 'On the contrary, I can, for as long as it takes.'

Her voice shook. 'To do what?'

'To convince you that I love you, that I can't let you go.'

For one long moment the floor seemed to lurch beneath her feet. She swayed and felt his arms go about her. His body was pressed, strong and hard against her own as he held her. He had said he loved her.

'But you can't. You don't. All you wanted was revenge, well you've had it, in full.'

His mouth tightened but it was sadness she saw in his eyes. 'I told myself the very same thing, but somehow saying it didn't make any difference. Oh, at first I may have wanted revenge but that was before I began to fall in love with you. I fought against it, I told myself you deserved to be hurt for what you'd done to Helga.'

'But . . . I didn't.' Her voice was little more than a whisper and he turned her face up to his and his mouth caressed her cheek, her lips.

'I know that now.'

She jerked away. 'I see. You've discovered the truth and now you've changed your mind, because I'm not and never was guilty?'

Savagely he caught her to him again and his mouth came down, silencing her. The strength of the kiss took her breath away and she swayed as he released her. 'No, that isn't why. Do you still believe that?'

She looked at him. 'No.'

He drew her closer, stroking the hair back from her face. 'Then why did you fight me? I wanted you.'

'And I wanted you, but I thought you were going to marry Helga. You let me believe it.'

'There was never any question of it. It was you I loved, even though you nearly drove me to distraction.'

'Is that why you forced me to come out here, to Austria?'

'How else could I be sure I wouldn't lose you?' His mouth found hers again, this time gentle then more and more demanding as her own responded. When they finally broke apart she looked up at him and shivered. 'And to think you so nearly did, and that I almost lost you.'

'But it won't happen again, my love, not if I have to keep you a prisoner here for ever.'

She sighed and relaxed against him. 'I would be a very willing prisoner.'

'But I have a better idea. I'll make you my wife. It seems the best solution and after all you'll be hopelessly compromised after we've spent the night together up here.'

She looked out of the window. 'I'm not compromised yet. Perhaps we could walk back to the village.'

'But it's snowing.'

She looked again. 'So it is.' With a sigh of happiness she went to his arms, surrendering herself to his kisses once again. 'I quite like the idea of being a spring bride.'

But he tilted her chin up. 'It may be a very long winter and I've no intention of waiting. I was thinking that perhaps next week, or is that too soon?'

'Not at all,' she murmured. 'After all, haven't we already wasted enough time?'

Two more Doctor Nurse Romances to look out for this month

Mills & Boon Doctor Nurse Romances are proving very popular indeed. Stories range wide throughout the world of medicine — from high-technology modern hospitals to the lonely life of a nurse in a small rural community.

These are the other two titles for August.

CHATEAU NURSE
by Jan Haye

After an attack of pneumonia, Nurse Hilary Hope jumps at the chance of doing some private nursing in France but does not expect her life to be turned upside down by the local devastating doctor there, Raoul de la Rue . . .

OVER THE GREEN MASK
by Lisa Cooper

An exciting new part of her life begins when Nurse Jennifer Turner first reports at the Princess Beatrice Hospital — but nothing works out as she'd dreamed after she meets handsome registrar, Nicholas Smythe.

On sale where you buy Mills & Boon romances.

The Mills & Boon rose is the rose of romance

Look out for these three great Doctor Nurse Romances coming next month

CARIBBEAN NURSE
by Lydia Balmain
Staff Nurse Coral Summers' new job in the Caribbean is the chance of a lifetime, but couldn't she somehow have stopped herself falling in love with the arrogant surgeon Philip Kenning?

NURSE IN NEW MEXICO
by Constance Lea
Nurse Tessa Maitland flies all the way to Santa Fé and meets her sister's attractive doctor, Blair Lachlan. But she finds it hard to tell if he strongly dislikes her or is madly in love with her . . .

UNCERTAIN SUMMER
by Betty Neels
Nurse Serena Potts is thrilled when Dutchman Laurens van Amstel proposes to her, but the problems begin when he tries to back out of their engagement . . .

On sale where you buy Mills & Boon romances.

The Mills & Boon rose is the rose of romance

The Mills & Boon Rose is the Rose of Romance

Every month there are ten new titles to choose from — ten new stories about people falling in love, people you want to read about, people in exciting, far-away places. Choose Mills & Boon. It's your way of relaxing:

August's titles are:

COLLISION by Margaret Pargeter
After the heartless way Max Heger had treated her, Selena wanted to be revenged on him. But things didn't work out as she had planned.

DARK REMEMBRANCE by Daphne Clair
Could Raina marry Logan Thorne a year after her husband Perry's death, when she knew that Perry would always come first with her?

AN APPLE FROM EVE by Betty Neels
Doctor Tane van Diederijk and his fiancée were always cropping up in Euphemia's life. If only she could see the back of both of them?

COPPER LAKE by Kay Thorpe
Everything was conspiring to get Toni engaged to Sean. But she was in love with his brother Rafe — who had the worst possible opinion of her!

INVISIBLE WIFE by Jane Arbor
Vicente Massimo blamed Tania for his brother's death. So how was it that Tania soon found herself blackmailed into marrying him?

BACHELOR'S WIFE by Jessica Steele
Penny's marriage to Nash Devereux had been a ' paper ' one. So why did Nash want a reconciliation just when Penny wanted to marry Trevor?

CASTLE IN SPAIN by Margaret Rome
Did Birdie love the lordly Vulcan, Conde de la Conquista de Retz — who wanted to marry her — or did she fear him?

KING OF CULLA by Sally Wentworth
After the death of her sister, Marnie wanted to be left alone. But the forceful Ewan McNeill didn't seem to get the message!

ALWAYS THE BOSS by Victoria Gordon
The formidable Conan Garth was wrong in every opinion he held of Dinah — but could she ever make him see it?

CONFIRMED BACHELOR by Roberta Leigh
Bradley Dexter was everything Robyn disliked. But now that she could give him a well-deserved lesson, fate was playing tricks on her!

If you have difficulty in obtaining any of these books from your local paperback retailer, write to:

Mills & Boon Reader Service
P.O. Box 236, Thornton Road, Croydon, Surrey, CR9 3RU.